GUARDiANS

Iain Mackenzie-Blair is the Scottish poet Ian Blake, past winner of the Neill Gunn and Petra Kenney Awards with four collections: *Aultgrishan, Waiting for Ginger Rogers at Loch Oich, Remembering Falstaff & Others, Disciplines of War* (2014). His previous novel *School Story* (2006) is currently an e-book trilogy: *I Drift, II Blood, III Fall.*

Of *SCHOOL STORY*

"This book is gripping from beginning to end....deserves to be much better known in the realm of public school stories and has all the hallmarks of a classic." *Front Free Endpaper*

"I read it straight through in two days...Like that Wordworthian crag seen at night 'a huge peak, black and huge' it dominated my mind for days, dark and wonderful, and I salute the author." *Northwords Now*

"It's chillingly convincing. ... What is so frightening about *School Story* is that, after the rites of initiation, you present the signs of hope and relief, the reaching after a more humane regime on the part of, say, Mawsom or Snider, the athletic triumphs, even academic successes, and we expect the prison doors, now slightly ajar, to open...then bang! wallop! they slam shut. No enlightened reform but the re-imposition of sadistic control by the pupils themselves, even the return of the Digger! Fidello turns into 1984..." *From a reader*

GUARDiANS

Are not two sparrows sold for a penny?
Yet not one of them will fall to the ground
apart from the will of your Father
Matthew 10:29-30

Iain Mackenzie-Blair

John & Eve
with best wishes,
the Author
Dec '18
Iain

THREE CATS PRESS

Copyright © Iain Mackenzie-Blair 2018
First published in 2018 by Three Cats Press
Aultgrishan
Wester Ross, IV21 2DZ
email: tcp@iambik.org

Distributed by Lightning Source

British Library Cataloguing in Publication Data
A catalogue record for this book is available from the British Library

All of the characters in this book are fictitious and any resemblance to
actual people, living or dead, is purely imaginary.

ISBN 978-0-9932171-0-4

Typeset by Amolibros, Milverton, Somerset
This book production has been managed by Amolibros
Printed and bound by Lightning Source

Acknowledgements

My thanks to Jens Andexer for putting me right about Canadian idiom (eg butts not fag-ends!), any remaining *betises* are mine. Jane Moores ran her eagle-eye over a first draft and related how marching ants ruined a party for her and Tig when they were children. Finally, my gratitude to Jane Tatam of Amolibros for her tactful editorial expertise preparing the text of *Guardians*.

I

JUNE

There's special providence in the fall of a sparrow...
...If it be now 'tis not to come; if it be not to come it will
be now...

1

On the twentieth of May, 'Pope' Potter doubled his congregation. He sat that Sunday, as he had most Sundays for as long as most people could remember, at the corner of McCutcheon Square, dirty white robe billowing beneath long grey hair tied in a straggly bun and crowned by a battered once black top-hat. While he dreamed and sang his way through his personal revelation, his knees pumped slowly away at the cranks of an incredibly ancient delivery tricycle as though he were attempting to ride his way into Paradise, but it did not move.

A makeshift lever, latched into position by a hank of much-reused string, nestled tightly against the curling nickel-plating of the handlebar and a limp brake. This lever, by means as mysterious as it was precarious, transformed the pedalling motion to the bellows of a chipped harmonium suspended on tired springs which spanned the area between the two front wheels. The top of the harmonium was dressed into the semblance of an altar.

Occasionally, on days when there had been a shower of rain and the weathered wooden frame was relatively clear of dust, the faintest trace of the original name and trade could be deciphered:

POTTER – FAMILY – BUTCHER

Nobody knew or cared whether the name referred to him, or whether he had merely scrounged it from a dump. Had anyone in Salter's Creek been asked, they would have said that 'Pope' Potter had arrived with the contraption for his first "service" in the dim and distant past, but when precisely that was would have been anyone's guess.

Air hissed and groaned from punctured bellows and bent pipes. Every so often the old man ran his hands over keys as filthy and discoloured as his long spatula fingers which were almost too thick to avoid pressing two keys at a time. He looked up always, into heaven and the correct stops and notes were discovered more by their rarity than his skill.

Discordant vestiges of familiar hymns or liturgical chants spilled out into the air. They were ghosts of tunes; music twisted almost out of recognisable shape, haphazard and fragmentary as the thoughts he preached and the words and phrases he used to express them. Sometimes one puncture larger than the rest allowed a momentary jet of air to dibble the dust beneath into a dimple and then the continuous groans and sighs were overburdened with a long, tooth-jarring whistle.

The altar cloth, a piece of red canvas embroidered by an eccentric frieze of old cord and string threaded into the shape of crosses, flapped up and down as the entire contraption wallowed on its springs like a becalmed paddle-boat.

Pope Potter seemed oblivious to all material inadequacy; on Sunday in McCutcheon Square, he communed with God. He sang and droned himself to an ecstasy, while his faithful, solitary listener blinked and dozed in the heady warmth.

"Wake, wake, ye sinful world and sing
Per-raise – the everrrlasting King,
Wake ye pee-pul, sin not – Sing
Praise to-oo God who-oo issss…the Kinnnnggggg."

His voice wavered from thin soprano into a harsh, astonishingly low bass. The sound drifted on a light wind. It curled down the long-abandoned street with its peeling-shuttered shops. Occasionally it seemed to be sung back in a muted echo from hot panes of filthy glass. Nothing stirred: Salter's Creek went to church on Sunday morning; Pope Potter's voice alone inhabited the untrodden alleys and long-sleeping verandas. Even at the farthest end of the town he could be heard fitfully. There was still almost an hour of the church service to go. Time edged its tedious way along drifts of sidewalk dust and ever present scatter of pine needles, measured out it seemed by an enormous brass-faced black clock which stood to one side of his 'altar' and registered the minutes as Pope Potter prayed them on their way.

"Li…*iiiiift* up…"

His congregation opened one eye, scratched first the right ear, carefully, then the left more vigorously, yawned, sneezed, settled once more into the warm dust. The air grew hot.

Then the dog barked.

It stood up immense and rangy, ragged black fur, feathers of the tail rising ominously. Short pointed ears which lay back along its head, white hairs fringing the tip of each gave it the appearance of an old man, snarling and impotent. Pope Potter stopped, jerked back into reality, legs remaining motionless, hands still on the keys. Air drained from the harmonium, music petered away in one long dying screech. He rubbed his eyes as if unable to believe what was left of his senses and then mopped his brow with the hem of grubby vestments made from once-white flour sacks stitched together by twine.

Pope Potter and the newcomer looked at each other across the sullen dog and the thick dust which furred the road, sun so nearly overhead that shadows were short and stubby. The bright light embraced them, an old man, a dog, dusty pavements, dilapidated shingled wooden buildings and a boy. Salter's Creek lay silent as a river bank before the first shots in a duel.

"Not in church!" The old man spoke half to himself, unbelievingly and then louder, almost accusingly, "You're not in church?"

The boy shrugged his shoulders and scuffed the dust with the toe of a shoe that looked as though it had been cleaned for church. He was about eleven, difficult to tell, skin tanned soft brown by sun in the open air, golden hair, high colouring, firm lips and straight nose.

"That's right." The boy looked-up when he spoke. "I don't *have* to go, do I?" His reply, neither aggressive nor subservient, a statement of fact.

"You don't *have* to go." The preacher repeated the phrase slowly, uncertainly, word by word. It was as if he were trying to work out something. He repeated the phrase again, "*You* don't have to go...*you don't* have to go..." the stress different each time. He looked at the boy narrowly as one might at a conjurer or a cheapjack salesman claiming extravagant qualities for his wares.

The boy was handsome. There was more to it than that. The old man looked round him. He saw as if for the first time drab cracked woodwork, sun-bleached paint, grimy panes of unused rooms above the boarded shops, registered for a fleeting second, his own grimy robes and the incongruous altar cloth. His fuddled mind was visited by a new understanding: *The boy was beautiful.*

That was it. He looked up, squinting into the sun. Or perhaps the boy only *seemed* beautiful. It was necessary to make sure. "Why haven't I seen you before?" The old man began to pedal again, but unconsciously; it was almost a reflex action.

"Don't know," the boy said, looking at the dog which continued to growl at the back of its throat. He pushed the soft dust into a heap and squidged it down with his toe.

"Name?"

"Kip."

"Kip? Hmmmm. Kip. Kip. Funny name?"

Pope Potter pedalled harder. A look of cunning came into his face, he looked at the boy out of the corner of his eyes. "What's you *real* name?"

"I *like* being called Kip," the boy said defiantly then, daunted perhaps by the authoritative tone, muttered diffidently "Christopher." His parents had called him Kit but, inability at an early age to pronounce the letter 't' meant he'd answer 'Kip' whenever asked his name. And it had stuck.

"Christopher…" the old man breathed, "*Christ…o…pher?*" nodding to himself as if it were something he should have known already. "Why not in church, heh? *Why not in church?*" He spoke in a hoarse conspiratorial whisper.

"Isn't this as good as going to the church?" looking up through his lashes without lifting his head.

The old man was uncomfortable. The boy might be making fun of him, grinning, pointing, like all the others. He had an idea that the boy's reply might somewhere contain a joke which he couldn't understand. His eyes began to water, a big tear cleaning a path through the dust on his cheek. Perhaps this beautiful boy was not quite what he had been seeking after all. "Where is your father?"

"My father's in Heaven."

It was as if he challenged the preacher to say anything different, but the weirdly robed figure was staring straight ahead of him.

"Ahhhh…Wake, Wake, Ye Sinful World and Sing," he intoned absentmindedly, the notes off-key, "God in Heaven is Our Kiiiii-nnng," terminating them with a long, low, chord on the harmonium complementing the growl of the dog. He stopped again. He was still not sure, not quite sure. He would have to think. The boy disturbed him. That much was certain. He would have to think about it and *why* the boy disturbed him. Thinking took time. He muttered aloud to himself, "Ye Shall Not Stay in Darkness at The Last Dawn."

"Well I'm going now, anyhow." Had the boy misunderstood him deliberately? Accidentally? "But," he said politely almost sympathetically "I'll bet it's the first time you've had an audience 'cept for..." nodding at the dog.

"Congregation," the old man interrupted fiercely. "*Congregation*! Congregation! *You* ought to know that if..."

Surprised at the vigour of it, the boy stuck his hands in the front pockets of his jeans which were still new enough for the copper rivets at the corners of the pockets to gleam in the light; his 'best', he wore them only on Sundays. Usually, like most of the others, he wore shorts and sneakers. "All right, sorry, I mean *congregation*. Anyway I was only goin' t'say I don't s'pose you ever have any 'congregation' except him." Gently with his foot he rolled a stone in the direction of the black dog which growled even more menacingly and half stood-up again. The remark was not made in a jeering manner, but as an observation worthy of record. Even Pope Potter could see that.

"G'bye," raising a hand in farewell. He sauntered off, hands back in his pockets scuffing the heels of his shoes in the dust which billowed up in a little cloud as though he left behind him a smouldering fuse. The old man's eyes stayed fixed on his back. Had the boy been making fun of him? He was not too crazed to realise that most of the others did. On the other hand, none of the others stayed away from church on Sunday to come and listen to him. Time had no part of it; the mere fact that the boy had been there at all was enough.

"*Isn't this as good as going to church?*"

The boy had said that. There was something else nagging at the back of his fuddled mind. It would be a matter of thinking it out; perhaps it was all connected with The Event he had been awaiting. What was The Event? The End Of The World? He had waited so long that he had forgotten; it would be necessary to think it out again. Who could tell? He leaned forgetfully on the keyboard and the harmonium squealed so agonisingly that the hackles on the dog began to rise again. The dog had not liked the visitor. Could that be a sign? Confirmation? However, the dog never liked any stranger.

The noise jerked the old preacher into speech. "Who Shall Behold the Beauty of The True God? None but the Blessed. None but the Blessed shall See His Face." His voice took on a chant. "Woe to Them who Fail to See the Door Divine. Happy Are They Who Meet Their God With Joy and Welcome."

The chant lingered, split itself into fragments idling down the half-built street which lodged its mouth at McCutcheon Square. Notes and disembodied words curled up into smart-curtained open windows above Parrotys Store, the only remaining commercial enterprise other than Mr Soong's modest laundry. They seemed to follow (or were they pursuing?) the boy as, dust muffling his footfalls, he dawdled past abandoned gardens and warped doors stretching and creaking in the early summer heat. They completed their lazy tour of the whole decayed township before finally teasing out amongst the first straggle of trees thus somehow accentuating the uncanny natural stillness of the morning.

"None but the *Blessed."* He was sure of that. The boy was beautiful – of that there could be no doubt. *Beautiful enough?* "Sing ye, Praise Go-o-o-" *Too beautiful?* Blue eyes fixed on the sky he sang high and wavering, the bellows wheezing so loud that sometimes his voice was completely drowned out "o-o-o-dd." *Too beautiful for what?* "O Ye Pee-pu-lll of Sin!" *How could he tell?*

The harmonium wheezed into silence, he stood high on the pedals and addressed a Congregation only he could see.

"Beware, Beware ye Children of Sin. The Beauty of Lucifer is the Ugliness of Everlasting Death," the words tolling into the bright air. Now, standing down beside his altar, he said it three more times while pulling on a pair of spotlessly white gloves.

With both hands he lifted above his head a 'chalice' fashioned from a tin once containing baked beans before reverently putting it to his lips and draining it in one swallow. Very slowly he peeled off the gloves, carefully folding them, restoring them to a battered biscuit tin, before clasping his hands so hard together that his face whitened beneath the tan. Sharp cheekbones stood out, throwing into shadowed relief the lined hollow cheeks and the yellowing straggle of white beard which trimmed his mouth and brushed the front of his crude vestment. He swayed to and fro, tears lumping unevenly over the creases in his face. "Let Not This Servant of His God Mistake the Hour," he wept to himself.

As abruptly as he had begun, he stopped, sat back on the tricycle and unlashed the twisted lever, pedalling furiously all the time, until with a grotesque retching sound the gear engaged and the machine lurched forward. Cumbersome, almost lethargic, it rolled down the slight incline. An axle squeaked. Usually everything was packed neatly away before moving but on the twentieth of May, Pope Potter had an appointment with his God which could not wait. The altar cloth flapped frantically and the black clock swayed heavily as the low-geared contraption gathered speed. Every so often a ratchet more tired and worn than the rest, slipped and Pope Potter pedalled even more furiously for an instant. Above his head, the banner that was normally packed away, still suspended between two broomsticks, billowed petulantly and twisted with a reproachful cracking sound, its faded lettering alternately looming and vanishing.

GOD IS TH E ON LY TR UE SOU RCE O F LI GHT

He had moved perhaps twenty yards and the rusty wheels

had settled into their customary muted protest when, suddenly remembering, he turned his body full on the seat.

"Get Thee Behind Me Satan."

The huge black dog, which had watched the old man's impending departure with almost malevolent incredulity, roused itself and loped along some yards behind adjusting to the speed of its master's vehicle so precisely and completely that it was as if it were attached by some invisible towing pole. They vanished together along the wide street in a lazy swirl of dust which obscured them both long before they disappeared from sight behind a distant bend in the road and the dark trees which stood awaiting them.

2

Hundreds of miles of wild, heavily forested land surrounded Salter's Creek, the relatively tree-free eminence around which wound the bed of a geologically long-dried river. Natural focus of the first-comers, itinerant French trappers, it had been little more than a trading post. Subsequently the surrounding area had been sparsely settled by waves of Scottish immigrants dispossessed of their tenancies because absentee landowners and their rapacious factors decided sheep were more profitable than poor farmers who could scarcely produce enough to support their families, let alone sell enough to pay rent on the few acres of peaty land they worked.

Macphersons, McLeods, McKays, wiry, tough men and women, implacably resentful that they had been driven from their traditional homeland, they had come and hacked out of virgin forest just enough cultivable land to support themselves and their families. From the trees they felled they constructed low windowless cabins almost as dark as the black-houses in which they had dwelt in the highland and islands before their forced migration. Lacking reeds or straw for thatching, they were roofed with rough-hewn planks which were then turfed, and draughty crevices between the logs packed with mud and moss until it seemed as if the dwellings themselves were some bizarre crop growing out of the very land that had been cleared.

As time passed many had been extended, some even storied or half-storied; small windows grudgingly lightened dark rooms, chimneys channelled smoke which had until then seeped out through the turf blackening roughly-adzed pine roof-beams.

Close and clannish, their descendants were just as tough, dour, still speaking among themselves a language no one but themselves understood. Sons and grandsons inherited the bitterness of the Highland Clearances which had forced them into exile.

On the outbreak of war in 1914 there had been only two who, enthused by early propaganda, slipped quietly away to join up. Their deaths in the mud on the first day of the Somme had been accepted even by their relations as little less than they deserved for volunteering to fight for a cause so dear to the very landlords who had deprived them of their true heritage in order to graze sheep.

The children, hardy as their parents, walked fearlessly through the forest to school, barefoot in summer, shabbily shod in cast-off boots during winter unless snow was too deep for even their stubborn determination; some had a two-hour journey out every morning and back each afternoon. At seasons of planting or harvesting, their labour valued more than books or learning, they might not appear for days at a time. Before sowing and after harvest their fathers supplemented their earning by trapping and selling the pelts. In the more remote farmsteads close to the distant river they felled and trimmed the towering pines, before rafting them down to the saw mills fifty miles away.

Relatively few of these once migrant families dwelt in Salter's Creek itself, however those who lived within a twenty-five- or thirty-mile radius regarded themselves as 'Creekers'– it was after all their postal address. According to the hand-written name on the creased much-foxed-sketch-map pinned to the wall of

Parrotys Store, the trading-post had been known originally as 'Three Pines Rough' although Pennery believed 'Rough' was due to mishearing the word 'Roche' in the original French trappers' translation of native-Indian name for Three Pines Rock.

The name itself became a matter of vigorous debate after Pennery's arrival. Loxton and the Parrotys had been told as children that towards the end of the nineteenth century the brothers Ben & Ezra Salter had discovered gold dust and even nuggets along the banks of the creek, which resulted in a much publicised gold-rush and a rapid influx of prospectors. *The Sentinel*, leading a campaign to establish a Founder's Day holiday, wondered why it had not been named McCutcheonville after the man who had been instrumental in developing a tiny trading post into a virtual township and after whom the square was named.

Increasingly tetchy ill-informed discussion was at its height when Pennery arrived. He suggested looking up or, to be more precise, getting looked up for them, some records, reputedly archived by a university in the east. These proved conclusively that, in fact, the name commemorated a notorious fraud. Halfway through the previous century, two 'prospectors', possibly brothers, surname unknown but certainly not Salter, turned up at the trading-post with evidence that they had struck gold. News spread and enticed the entire membership of a small, exclusive, religious sect who believed that the world would end on a day which would be revealed only to their charismatic leader. Declaring, "I am Divinely inspired to lead you, His Chosen Flock, to enjoy The Earthly Riches Your Dedication Deserves," he persuaded them to sell-up their city homes, pool the money and follow him. They arrived, bought every claim the two had registered and, now smugly wealthy, settled down to build a church and await the End of The World.

It came the morning they awoke to find that, under cover

of darkness, their esteemed leader had departed together with his deputy's wife, the rest of the sect's funds and the two 'prospectors' who had obviously arrived carrying the gold with which they had 'salted' their bogus claims. Disillusioned, having lost not only their money and their labour but also their faith, the community disintegrated and, like most of those who had flocked to the area on news of the supposed 'strike', drifted away leaving embryonic streets lined by unroofed un-finished houses to the elements. In view of this Pennery had light-heartedly advocated the introduction of an apostrophe which, to his surprise and amusement, had been adopted officially by Loxton and everyone except the editor of *The Sentinel*.

Half a mile or so from McCutcheon Square, the rocky eminence still known as 'Three Pine Rough', highest point on the promontory, was crowned by three giant redwoods which had established themselves many centuries back when the river still flowed and there had still been soil cover enough to encourage young saplings to root themselves deep into natural fissures. There they remained, leaning as if for mutual support, so close together that the very tops embraced each other at the apex; from a distance it looked like three intertwined poodle tails, or some extraordinary piece of topiary. All the lower and most of the middle branches having long vanished, this ungainly giant tripod could, for many years, be climbed only by those wearing the toe-spiked boots of professional lumberjacks. Then it had become a playground for boys to swing themselves hand-over-hand along ropes twisted round the three trunks, until it was decided that, situated as it was on the rocky knoll which was not merely the highest point in Salter's Creek but the highest point in the forest for over fifty miles, the trees would provide ideal 'legs' for supporting a fifty-foot high triangular fire-watching platform. A framework had been lashed to the now branchless trunks, this being floored with stout planks and enclosed on two sides by waist-high safety rails, to one of which was secured a substantial sophisticated three-pulley block-and-tackle.

Installed initially to lift timber for constructing the platform, it was re-installed each wild-fire 'season' in order to haul-up three heavy loudspeakers and the amplification equipment which enabled duty fire-watchers to alert members of the emergency squads wherever they were working during the day and rousing them at night. It remained in place 'for the duration' so that the weighty lead-acid batteries could be regularly exchanged and recharged. Human access was provided by two heavy wooden ladders; the lower one was removed from its iron hooks each autumn because if left in place throughout the winter it tempted adventurous children to dare each other 'to climb the tower'.

From the platform it was possible to look in every direction without discovering a break in the trees. Certainly there were isolated outlying homesteads but these were not large enough to disturb the dark green blanket. Trees grew everywhere they were not physically prevented from growing. In the spring they came up in gardens, beneath floorboards, pushed through road surfaces and were a constant problem in the graveyard. It was only because of its elevation on its knob of volcanic rock where the soil-cover was particularly thin, that Salter's Creek managed to hold the trees at bay just enough to keep it looking more like an embryonic township than a populated forest glade.

Despite the revelation that the name Salter's Creek was an ironic reference to past gullibility and fraud, the term *Creek* was cherished with affectionate humour precisely because there was now no sign of water. Mothers, ordering grubby children to give themselves a thorough wash might well tell them "Go bathe in the Creek". Whilst to say that somebody had 'swum Salter's

Creek both ways' was a way of saying the man in question was a damned liar.

Pennery declared there had indeed been a river flowing once upon a time. He said it first in a talk to the Church Ladies Group soon after he had arrived. He had taken his audience up to Three Pines Rough and pointed out how the now dry, rocky, treeless channel that curled round the township meandered "forming what was once an 'oxbow-lake'. Salter's Creek would have been virtually an island in the geological past when a river had flowed but," Pennery explained, "it vanished when the water-table dropped."

Few had anything but the haziest conception of an 'oxbow-lake' or indeed a 'water-table', but a well-shaft bored down fifty feet almost anywhere tapped into water that was sweet and plentiful at all seasons. So there was no reason to doubt Pennery who seemed a pleasant enough fellow; being the schoolmaster helped, it was his job to know things like that. After his famous lecture and the subsequent report of it in *The Sentinel,* Pennery's vanished river and 'oxbow-lake' became the town 'sight'. If ever relations arrived, which was rare, or a tourist, which was rarer still, they would be taken to view the dry channel. There was nothing else to see except trees. If the inhabitants joked amongst themselves about their *creek* they were proud of it too; it was a respectable local eccentricity.

McCutcheon Square was formed by the crossing at right angles of two wide, unpaved, half-built streets with balustraded wooden broad-walks broken only by sets of wide wooden steps at Parrotys Store and the long-barred-up swinging half-doors of what had been Lucky Strike beer-parlour. Although a few of the structures surrounding the square itself had been completed, most of those in the never-finished streets were empty. All had been battened against the fierce autumn winds which forced dust from the unsurfaced road into every available crack and crevice, dutifully weathering the wood to a Presbyterian grey. The vivid red, green, or blue doors of the few still occupied seemed brashly disrespectful if not positively irreverent. One or two which had been scarcely started, wooden-frames skeletally gaunt, stood there as if in reproach at their abandonment.

On one side of the square the sidewalk culminated at steps to the neglected but still dominating police-station which had been necessitated by the inrush of those lured by their dream of finding gold. PARROTYS STORE, still spick and span, efficiently run by the Misses Parroty, had been set up by grandfather McCutcheon. On news of the gold strike, he had driven west in his covered wagon, bought out the ramshackle trading-post and built a two-storey emporium to supply food and tools for the hundreds of hopeful prospectors staking claims all along the creek. He was accompanied by wife and pretty daughter. Shortly after their arrival, she had 'married' (at a distressingly young age) Joseph Parroty, a charming but feckless prospector who vanished, never to be seen again when the gold proved to be a fraudulent fiction, leaving his 'wife' to die giving birth to twin daughters. The store had survived by supplying the dour Scottish homesteaders and a few defeated but stubborn incomers who sustained themselves and their families as best they could once they faced up to the harsh reality that there had never been any gold.

McCutcheon Square was where people met; at Parrotys Store, at the shabby clapboard church on the far side, or at the laundry owned and operated by the seemingly ageless Mr Soong whose enigmatic silence suggested that he had very little English, although he seemed to understand perfectly those who brought blankets and eiderdown for his attention at winter's end. There was not even (and this was a peculiarity) a post office. Such mail as went out and came in on the weekly carrier was left to be claimed from boxes racked up at Parrotys.

Salter's Creek did not go out of its way to cater for, or bother to encourage, casual visitors. Such 'Hotel' accommodation as there was above the long-abandoned Lucky Strike was entered by a shabby side door and serviced by the Parroty sisters. Most of those who came by chance took one look and left as soon as they could, others who stayed a few months before drifting on took over one of the boarded-up houses with the acquiescence of Loxton and Randall; nobody any longer knew who or where the owners were.

Thus it was that Salter's Creek had the air of a settlement that had never really quite grown up, more impressive as a name on a map than in the actuality of its urban pretension; a township that, never having developed beyond its adolescence so to speak and had not merely given up the struggle to expand but was even too dispirited to fail dramatically. Most of those who did not leave stayed only because either geographically, spiritually, or both they could no longer be bothered to go any further: Salter's Creek had become the sort of place where people ended up.

Pennery had arrived one late-spring day shortly after the end of the War-To-End-All-Wars in the vehicle which brought the bank messenger and the post once a week. He said he was the new teacher and moved his sparse luggage into the schoolhouse. The previous incumbent had gone on vacation the previous summer and, without any explanation, never returned with the result that the school had ceased to function for almost a year.

Although Pennery was a graduate of one of England's great universities, nobody asked to see his credentials: who would dream of setting up as the schoolmaster in a place as remote as Salter's Creek unless he had been appointed by some faceless deskbound functionary in city offices hundreds of miles away? His quiet self-reliance and courteous reserve, even with those he taught aroused nothing except respect. He seemed somehow always within himself and, without anyone knowing quite why, it was generally assumed that he'd fought in France.

Patterson, after an early disagreement with the schoolmaster observing that he had arrived, "ink scarcely dry on the Armistice agreement", implied he was probably a 'conchie', even a deserter who had fled to Canada and "hidden himself away at Salter's Creek" – a phrase ironically perhaps more revealing of himself than Patterson realised.

The slur never stuck because nobody in the community, other than the two dead Scottish boys, had involved themselves in that bloody conflict; most of them secretly applauded someone who'd apparently had the sense to distance himself from the sickening slaughter, looking with positive approval on anyone who refused to fight for the country which had dispossessed their forefathers.

3

The Sunday Pope Potter doubled his congregation was not in any way memorable for most of those who lived in, or reasonably close to Salter's Creek. The Reverend Patterson was an exception; he noticed with irritation that Kip Harrison had not attended church with Pennery. The only other regulars who had cause to remember were one or two who were conscious of the fact that it was the seventh Sunday of the seventh week without rain. Summers were always dry at Salter's Creek, but already it seemed to have been dry much earlier than usual to those who thought about it.

"Anyhow it won't make any difference to the water supply, thank God." The tall man turned towards the chair on the veranda. Scent from a sweet and tantalising shrub drifted in from the garden. "But it'll play hell with our neighbours." Neighbours were over fifty miles to the east at Cranston where rafted-down timber was loaded onto railway waggons. Far larger than Salter's Creek, it was always in trouble in times of drought; Pennery said the underlying rock was 'porous'.

"Well it's a blessing it never makes any difference here. Never has done. Never!" Loxton twisted the thick glass tumbler between stubby fingers.

"Never has done what, Henry?" A woman emerging from the door behind them came across and joined in. She was smart and neat in contrast to the bulky, untidy man with crumpled jacket and creased collar who turned towards her without getting up from the chair. Her clothes delineated her sharply in an almost uncanny way, as though there were no knap to the cloth. Partially it was a trick of the fading light but, at any one instant, she seemed completely defined: it was always possible to see, so to speak, exactly where she began and where she ceased. Bella Loxton performed this function of definition for them both.

It was one of Loxton's amusements to remark tongue-in-cheek that he must be the longest serving 'Mayor' in the world, "Elected at the age of seven!" His grandfather, Henry Loxton, had been sent by central government to Salter's Creek at the time of the supposed gold strike in order to register claims, collect taxes and levies, register births and deaths, license firearms, provide trapping permits, as well as performing other official functions which accrued as the township started to flourish. These duties had been taken over by Loxton's father who had wooed Catriona Mair, daughter of one of the Scottish settler families. Her father, proud of his heritage, only agreed to the match on condition that his family name should be incorporated by deed-poll. Thus it was when their seven-year-old son was asked his name on his first day at school, he had piped up, "Henry Mair-Loxton."

The schoolmaster of the time, whose reputation for sarcasm was as richly deserved as that for taking the slightest excuse to applying stick or strap to pupils of either sex, paused, pen poised over the Register. "Is it indeed?!" He had no truck whatever with what he dismissed as 'pretentious affectations of gentility'. "Well as far as this *school* is concerned you are H. Mair," and wrote it down before turning to the class, "So boys and girls, we at last have here in Salter's Creek a little *Lord Mayor* at last!" He paused, "Well, '*Mister* Mayor' say hullo to your fellow citizens. Speak up now, Mair."

It was hardly surprising that, fearing the schoolmaster might turn on them, his contemporaries laughed, thereafter sycophantically referring to him as 'Mr Mayor', but it had long since become widely adopted as a term of genuine affection which would have incensed his long-dead schoolmaster. Newcomers, such as there were, assumed that it was his official title, not least because he had in due course taken over from his father all the administrative responsibilities which had accrued over the years even though Salter's Creek had never expanded into the populous township it had once promised to become.

Left to himself, Loxton's personal life and his 'official' duties would have merged, but Bella outlined the precise boundary of their private life and his public one for him. Without her unobtrusive separation of official from social events, 'Mayor' Loxton would have muddled through a 'privately-public' existence which would have certainly neutralised him as an effective and objective administrator. She tinkled crisp ice in her orange juice, holding the glass lightly and delicately between fingers as thin and delicate as his were thick and short.

"Oh, I was just saying that the drought never affected the water here."

"We're lucky."

"But," interposed the taller man, idly, "it makes the fire risk absolute hell." He nodded out at the dark forest stretching away into the distance. "Each day without rain those trees get drier and drier. Then one afternoon some fool comes along and drops a match or throws down a cigarette butt and we have to pay the penalty. When it dries as early as this the risk's increased enormously."

A little dumpy woman who had been there all the time, unmoving, came up and put an arm through his. "Don't worry about it, Dill!" She had a capable face and voice. "You've taken every precaution and now that we've cleared the trees such a long way out from the town itself, at least we should be safe even if the whole forest went up from here to Cranston." She wore a woolly skirt and an even woollier cardigan so that she contrasted utterly with the other woman. The fuzziness of her dark cardigan and skirt seemed to blend into the shadows of the veranda, playing tricks with the fading light and according her a disembodied, almost spectral appearance, only face and arms distinct.

"I don't think you've too much to worry about this year, Dill. We're better off than ever before. Plenty of voluntary fire-watchers too." Loxton nodded out to the tower at Three Pines Rough.

"Oh yes, I know that," the tall man sighed. "But it's never easy to get an emergency squad to the place of the fire. It need be only a fragment of glass in a small clearing under a strong sun for a few moments and we're off. And if it's a careless camper? Or a tramper? They don't bother to keep to paths, let alone the roads as you know. What really terrifies me – always has – is that if we have one big squad out and there's another fire which necessitates sending out the stand-by, then we're sunk; no reserves if either gets out of control. What do we do? Use everyone on one blaze and get it out quickly, then move on, or split forces? That takes at least twice as long. The trouble is there's no time to go out, have a look and get back…. If only we could use those field radios they had in the last years of the war but in amongst these blasted trees they're out of range after half a mile or so."

"*A policeman's lot…*" the neat woman hummed and moved to join the two of them at the veranda rail, leaving her husband still in his chair. Loxton heaved himself up and lumbered over, surprisingly he was hardly less tall than the policeman, yet his huge shoulders and bulky body, together with the enormous flapping trousers that he habitually wore, made him seem, at first glance, far the shorter of the two. During his younger days he had been one of the most physically powerful men in Salter's Creek even now, in middle age, he was still impressive when he pulled himself upright.

It was generally believed that the Loxtons once 'had money'. However it was also rumoured that the Wall Street crash had swallowed most of their savings, drastically reducing any income apart from what he earned as the administrating representative for the government in Ottawa.

"Don't *worry*, Dill. It'll probably never happen." The *cliché* hung in the soft air, ugly and unnecessary. His wife winced slightly, but she was used to him; he always meant what he said, however hackneyed the phraseology. The others noticed nothing unusual.

"What about a more cheerful topic for a conversation?" Bella Loxton turned to the policeman, "Come on Dill Randall!" she said, smiling. "What's the news? I've always been told that a good policeman should know everything. What dastardly deeds have come to light today?"

"On a Sunday? At Salter's Creek?" The tall man rolled his glass between fingers and thumb and looked at them. "To my knowledge there's only one dastardly deed happens here on a Sunday what's more it's every Sunday," he paused, "and that's a regular crime."

"The Reverend Patterson's sermon!" they chorused, laughing. It was not a particularly original joke, but they were his friends.

Loxton regarded them benevolently as might a jolly doctor about to tell a patient that he was all but cured. "*Un*-officially of course," sipping his drink and inferring mock 'Mayoral' dignity by adding, "perhaps I should run my next election campaign on the ticket of getting rid of Patterson's sermon?" The self-deprecating references to his supposed election was as familiar an element in their light-hearted discussion as the length of Patterson's sermons.

"My dear Henry if there *were* elections and you stood on *that* platform, anyone who thought of opposing you would probably be lynched," Randall concluded.

"But," began the plump little woman, "The Reverend Patterson's sermon is hardly news, even if it is a crime."

"In that case," her husband answered lightly, running his finger down the side of his nose, "if that's not news then there's even less news than crime this Sunday in Salter's Creek."

"I believe," Loxton said pontifically, "that you're holding back on us. I saw you talking very earnestly to Special Constable Oates. Come on 'give', as we old newspaper men are supposed to say."

"Well, Henry," the policeman began to tick items off on his fingers, "apart from the fact that I doubt even your articles in *The Sentinel* telling us what the local rates and taxes pay for make you an 'old newspaperman' there are three very shocking items I suppose I ought to report. Last night," he began, looking round conspiratorially, "dear *Kennethina!*" Randall paused dramatically (Kennethina ailurophilic widow of Humphrey Biggelowe who had owned and run the declining Lucky Strike and Hotel until it finally closed at the outbreak of the war, only child of Macpherson parents who, disappointed that it had not been a son, had in the Highland way given her the feminised name of her paternal grand-father), before resuming in his normal voice, "*Mrs* Kennethina Biggelow, well She-Lost-Her-Key…" investing every word with equal emphasis, "*Again!* She came down to call her beloved cat. The door slammed on her and there she was locked out. Fortunately Special Constable Oates happened to be passing on his way home, heard her call and glanced over the fence. She slipped rapidly into the barn and…"

"And he climbed in through a window and opened the door?"

"Not at once. She was only wearing her nightie and wouldn't

even let him come into the garden until she had hidden behind the woodpile, refusing to leave the barn until he'd left."

"Did he?"

"No, he told her not to be so silly and turned his back…"

"And…?"

"She invited him in for a cup of tea… . And guess what he saw?"

"Her red flannel?"

"No, her hair was 'in papers', that's why she was shy it seems. But what he saw round her neck on a piece of blue ribbon was her front door key. Where, she told him, she always keeps it."

"That," said Loxton, "is a *really* nasty business. What we'd do without our police I just can't think. I must make a note of it for my history of Salter's Creek. Anything else?"

"Well…this morning there was *real* excitement. The Harrison boy played hookey from church."

"Bet his father'll tan his ass for that," said Loxton, despite a protest from his wife, "him being a churchwarden."

"Oh no, not *Harris*. Not *Adam's* boy. That poor kid wouldn't dare be *late* for church let alone skip it. I mean young Harris*on*."

"Kip?"

"Yes, young Kip Harrison."

"Skipped, did he? Good for him. An example for us all. Wish I dared do the same." There was a touch of genuine regret in Loxton's voice.

"I wonder if that's why he didn't want to go to the Pattersons? A dislike of church?"

"Or of Patterson?" the policeman said thoughtfully. "I knew that lad had character," he went on, "to turn down Patterson in the definite way he did."

"More than I can do," Loxton said ruefully. "That man comes into my office, looks across at me, mutters something about wood-beetle in the steps to the organ loft and the pulpit, insisting

'It's a *community* responsibility…' and I just give in, back him up, make a grant from the Rate. Anyhow the kid's absence'll probably annoy Patterson."

"I'm pretty sure the boy didn't mean it like that, certainly nothing vindictive… . Probably thought it was too good a morning to waste…don't blame him either. I s'pose living with his aunt he probably hasn't yet realised that *everyone* goes to church if they live not too far away – unless they're ill!"

"I'll take a bet that Patterson complains to Pennery," Loxton insisted doggedly.

"Is this the boy who lost his aunt?" Edith Dill queried.

Loxton nodded. "We only call him Harrison because that was her name. His parents' name was…d'you know I have to confess I can't remember."

Bella Loxton suggested tentatively, "Perhaps it was Harrison too…if she was the sister of the boy's father…but I have an idea she might have been the father's aunt, the boy's great aunt."

"Well he's a nice-looking boy." She gazed out into the night. "Dill and I would have liked a boy like that when… . First his parents then his great aunt…" Then, almost to herself, "Mind you she was a good age."

"I hear she trained in nursing? Or was driving ambulances? Mesopotamia? Certainly the Western Front in the last years of the war?"

Soon after Miss Harrison had returned to Salter's Creek, not long before Pennery's arrival, her father the long-time resident doctor had died in the flu epidemic and, in consultation with the nearest doctor, Svenssen at Cranston, she had taken over treatment of all minor ailments and less serious accidents.

"Curious the boy choosing his schoolmaster," Bella Loxton mused.

"Wouldn't have done in my day," her husband laughed.

Edith Randall said thoughtfully, "I can't understand what it is about Pennery but he wins everyone over. I'm not surprised young Kip chose him."

"Well, he certainly hasn't won over Patterson," the neat woman joined in.

"But my dear Bella," her husband turned to her, "in small communities schoolmaster and Minister are always on opposite sides of the fence. I'd be worried if they weren't," he finished triumphantly.

Bella Loxton was not defeated. "I'm not at all sure that the boy mightn't have been much better-off with the Pattersons. A married couple would be more...suitable. Two...Proper Parents." She spoke with conviction.

"I back *you* up, Henry," Randall challenged back. "The boy's perfectly all right with Pennery and he'll be a credit to us. I'll keep an eye on him to see he doesn't get into mischief, we all will. He has the whole of Salter's Creek looking out for him."

"You men always stand by each other," Bella Loxton said, laughing.

There was a pause. Then Edith Randall said, "Come on, Dill, you haven't told us the third thing yet."

"The third thing? Ah, the third piece of news. Well it's just this, Pope Potter went home early today."

"So he did," Bella Loxton paused, glass half-lifted. "Now I remember that he wasn't about his usual packing-up when we crossed the square after church."

"But there are Sundays Pope Potter never comes, aren't there?"

"No, not really. He does sometimes push off early, but unless the rain is pouring down he always at least *begins* his 'service'. And he was certainly arriving when we came across McCutcheon Square on the way to church."

Loxton pretended to look thoughtful. "A very serious business this. *Who did what to Pope Potter!*"

"He stayed there for a time. I know that," said Randall. "Something sent him off earlier than usual. I saw him pedalling away as though the devil himself were after him, banner flapping…he didn't even pack up today. That damned great black dog was lolloping along after him as usual."

"Perhaps he's seen the light and has come to his senses," his wife remarked. "I mean he really is very odd sometimes."

"I think it's much more likely that he was taken short and made for the trees," laughed Loxton.

"Really Henry," his wife began in pretended shock at her husband's streak of vulgarity, "I think you ought to show a modicum of self-control when…" But her turn of phrase in the context of the previous remark was more than unfortunate and there was more laughter.

Eventually, the laughing having subsided, Edith Randall, who had been thinking about other things during the joking, said, "I sometimes wonder if we ought not to do something about Pope Potter… . He isn't quite…all there…in the head… . You know what I mean…and…well…if he hurt somebody, or even hurt himself, it would be our fault."

"In a way you're right, Edith," replied the other woman, "but you and I know the old boy would be unhappy in a Home for… . Anyhow there isn't anywhere within hundreds of miles."

"You two women are always fussing needlessly." Loxton poured drinks all round. "Pope Potter's as well off here as anywhere. He lives somewhere out there in the forest which he likes. People are always giving him flour, eggs and milk and we're a reasonable bunch of people who can deal with him much better than any organisation. It's the same with Kip Harrison, they'll be looked after by everyone, both of them. Even the amount of freedom offered by a man like Pennery can give is, well – circumscribed by the very fact that this is the sort of community it is." He paused and thought back on their conversations, "We're all, each one of us, guardians of them both."

"That's all very well, Henry, but say something happens so that we can't look after either of them? That's why I think the boy needs two proper parents. Everything's all right now, but what if there were…a war for instance or…or…?"

"An attack by '*Injuns*'?" They all laughed. The policeman had put his finger on Bella Loxton's weakness which was Western films. However ancient they might be, she always sat spellbound whenever they were shown.

"Inspector Randall, as your 'Mayor' I'll not have you making fun of my wife," Loxton said with mock formality. "And, incidentally, how does it happen that you saw Pope Potter pushing off down the road and we saw nothing when we came out of church? Did you by any chance sneak off early?"

Edith Randall laughed, "Oh Dill, that *has* let the cat out of the bag – after all these years too!"

"Discovered!" her husband hissed theatrically. "Caught in the act! You know, Henry, you ought to have been a detective. As a matter of fact I was on duty. Guarding the town from evildoers."

"That," said Loxton slowly, thoughtfully, "must be why you always sit at the back. Yet you're always there when I come for the collection."

"Duty, duty, all in the course of duty."

"If you're there at Collection time," Bella Loxton said thoughtfully, "yet you're always there at the end…" She stopped. "It must mean…you're away for—"

"The Reverend Patterson's sermon!" they chorused together.

"I'd never have thought it of you, Dill." Loxton laughed. "I must say that if I were you I'd be ashamed to have pretended all these years that I'd been at the sermon."

"My dear Henry, I've never *pretended* anything of the sort.

You've always assumed it. Anyway you'd do the same if you had a chance."

"Must be great fun being a policeman," Loxton snorted.

"You're just jealous."

"I am, too true I am." The big man shivered. "It's getting cold, let's have a last drink inside." He turned through the barely discernible doorway, there came a click in the still air and a comfortable yellowish glow poured out into the gathering darkness. The two women sauntered through the door, one a clean-cut silhouette, the other plump and furrily indistinct. Dill Randall stretched and followed. The door shut on the darkness and the trees. Somewhere amongst them Pope Potter prayed for guidance.

Back in the schoolhouse Kip Harrison was surprised to learn that his absence had been noticed, let alone critically commented on. It had been no deliberate gesture, merely the result of being slightly delayed by last-minute shoe-cleaning. Finding the service already begun, shy of entering late, he'd preferred not to try to sneak in when he would surely have been noticed by eagle-eyed Young Miss Parroty in her organ-loft eyrie. While living with his aunt they had not attended regularly and, although she had never said as much to him, Pennery suspected she had little regard for Patterson's sanctimonious pronouncements from the pulpit.

Thus it was that nobody except the boy and the old man knew of their chance encounter; even had the whole town known it would have barely been thought remarkable. However, in the light of subsequent events it was perhaps a pity that Kip never thought it worth mentioning their meeting to Pennery, let alone relating their conversation such as it was.

4

i

Bella Loxton questioning Pennery's suitability as a guardian was not motivated by personal antipathy as was Patterson's. Although the loose ward-ship Pennery offered was certainly safeguarded by the interest and the concern of a small close community, she understood that a boy of his age, deprived of the affection first of parents and now of the great aunt he had come to love, might need something more personal, more intimate than the schoolmaster was willing to offer. She divined intuitively that for some reason Pennery seemed unable...no, reluctant...to take on responsibility for somebody else's welfare – as if it were too painful, too burdensome for him to embark on even the most fleeting emotional tie. *Was that why he had never married? Divorced perhaps?* However, although her intuition was not keen enough to define her reservations more precisely, she sensed that the 'freedoms' for the boy which her husband endorsed would be safely circumscribed by the affectionate goodwill of the community only as long as the way of life at Salter's Creek pursued its familiar undramatic routine.

There are some children who are veterans. Kip Harrison's parents had died on a splendid summer evening in a car smash caused by the drunk driver of a vast articulated oil tanker who escaped unscathed. Barely eight years old, concussed and badly cut, he had been extricated by an intrepid passing motorist minutes before the wreckage was engulfed in flame. The only relative who could be traced, an elderly aunt of his father whom he had never previously met, had travelled half a continent to collect him from the hospital to which he had been admitted. In the way bad things happen, barely three years after his arrival, she died naturally and peacefully in her bed leaving him parentless once again.

Salter's Creek still retained the ethos of the original frontier settlement it had been the century before. Too small a community to be sentimental, they accepted the charge that lay upon them. A suddenly parentless child was not an altogether unfamiliar situation There was never any question of an orphanage even had the nearest been situated closer than two hundred miles. As far as the adults could observe Kip was popular enough with his contemporaries although, unlike others of his age, he seemed to have no close or special friends. The boy seemed in no way 'difficult' or 'troubled' but rather on the quiet side which was understandable in the circumstances.

In many ways the whole of Salter's Creek was his home, but the practical problem of precisely where, day by day, he should eat and sleep and who specifically should be responsible for him had to be resolved. Within two days of his aunt's funeral, during which time the Randall's had given him a bed, Patterson had proposed that he and his wife should look after the boy permanently.

"That's a very good idea!" Loxton had enthused, relieved that the matter should have settled itself so quickly. "It's an ideal solution. Thank you very much…an *ideal* solution! I'll get hold of Kip and ask if it's OK by him."

Patterson was astonished there should be any suggestion that the boy himself might be consulted. He had agreed only because he was too taken aback to raise any immediate objection. As he saw it, the only rights children possessed were those exercised on their behalf by adults.

Loxton had no idea how much his decision had jolted the Minister. According to his own way of thinking, he had done nothing remarkable. Childless himself, he assumed children were basically equals who would no more appreciate being 'managed' without being consulted than he himself would have been even at Kip's age. It had never occurred to Loxton that Patterson expected to be handed the boy there and then like a parcel without Kip having, or being entitled to have, any say in the matter – not that was there any doubt in his mind that Kip would gladly accept Patterson's offer. A quaint and perhaps unusual regard for personal dignity had made him wise: it was surely up to each individual, man, woman or child, to decide for themselves, even if their decision was entirely predictable.

The following day, Loxton, seeing the boy crossing McCutcheon Square after school had finished, called Kip into his office and told him of the proposal. "Think it over, son. Then come back and let me know as soon as you can." Imagining the whole business had been settled, he telephoned Patterson, who had already told his wife that he would have the room at the top of the house next to next to their own bedrooms his and his wife's bedrooms re-decorated for the boy.

Two days later, Kip Harrison walked into the office again, just before Loxton started out for lunch. "All OK, son? I gather Pattersons are looking forward to having you, so when are…?" when Kip politely interrupted.

"I've made up my mind if that's what you mean, Mr Loxton,

sir." The boy spoke with a certain slow deliberation though without hesitation. "It's very kind of the Reverend and Mrs Patterson..."

"They're kind folks, Kip."

"Yes. Mr Loxton, but all the same I'd like to stay with Mr Pennery if you don't mind. Would that be all right?"

It would be too much to say Loxton was astonished, surprised perhaps but in no way disconcerted. Although hardly what he had expected, it seemed a perfectly reasonable alternative solution. After all Pennery was the boy's schoolmaster and the adult with whom he'd most come into contact apart from his aunt. Moreover, it now came back to him that he had more than once seen her talking to Pennery.

Not long after the new schoolmaster had arrived, he remembered Bella saying, from something she had overheard, that it was possible Pennery had come across Miss Harrison when she was nursing out there on the Western Front. *Perhaps that's when Pennery had first heard of Salter's Creek?* He recalled Patterson's 'conchie' slur. Even had Pennery been a conscientious objector then, Loxton supposed, he might well have been a stretcher-bearer at a forward-aid post. It would account for the first-aid expertise he'd demonstrated when a child had tripped and fallen on a protruding rock just after school one afternoon. Bad wartime experiences might explain Pennery's personal reticence and he had the large schoolhouse, ample room there for both of them. Pennery was unmarried, however the extremely efficient but partially deaf elder Parroty sister, Egeria, who took care of the everyday running of Parrotys Store and the rarely used 'hotel' accommodation, such as it was above the now defunct Lucky Strike Saloon, also acted as part-time housekeeper for Pennery; a familiar figure stomping round the schoolhouse, silver ear-trumpet on its elaborate chain round her neck.

When Loxton reflected on the matter later he had to admit that given the choice, had he been Kip, he too might have chosen the amiable schoolmaster as his guardian rather than the austere Minister.

"Is that you, Pennery?" he called into the phone after the customary whispering and crackling had died away a little, for it was a notoriously bad line. "How soon can young Kip to move in with you?"

"Young Kip?"

"Harrison, Kip Harrison."

"Old-Miss-Harrison-who-died-last-week's-nephew?" Pennery sounded at a loss.

"It's OK then? You'll be the boy's official guardian of course."

"Guardian? I'm not sure what you mean."

"Young Kip says he wants to stay with you. Is that OK?"

There was a pause. "Are you sure?"

"It's not *me* who's sure, Pennery, it's the *boy*," Loxton laughed, mildly surprised at Pennery's initial blankness over the boy's name. "The kid's happy with things arranged that way."

"Well, of course then. There's plenty of room here. You can count on me to do my best to make him welcome."

Nobody, least of all Loxton, realised the truth of the matter was that Kip himself had made the decision without consulting Pennery. Nor did Pennery say that it was the first he had heard anything about the matter. He assumed it was something the community as a whole had agreed, taking his willingness to co-operate for granted. He was in no way offended that it had all been arranged by Loxton and others, presumably because the schoolhouse had plenty of accommodation, although it crossed his mind to wonder why the Pattersons had not been chosen; they too had plenty of room and it was common knowledge that Joyce Patterson would have liked a child.

As for Leonard Patterson, in his own mind there had been

no question but that the boy would come to them. Loxton's call rendered him momentarily speechless. Kip's decision crystallised his long resentment of Pennery. It was inconceivable that there was any explanation other than the obvious one: the schoolmaster had somehow persuaded the boy to choose him as guardian in order to spite Patterson: a public affront to him both as man and Minister. Nothing could be done immediately; Patterson was canny enough to realise that making an issue of the affair would succeed only in broadcasting his own humiliation. Therefore he waited. Kip's absence from church some weeks later was to provide the first opportunity to pursue a legitimate grievance.

Kip himself would have been unable to articulate the reason he had chosen Pennery. It was neither a well-defined like of Pennery, nor an active dislike of the Pattersons which guided him, indeed he rather liked Joyce, although he had met her only three or four times at his great aunt's house. Partially it may have been the first stealthy, unrecognised, approach of adolescence that led him instinctively to adopt a course that would allow him to develop his own personality unrestricted by ties of affection that might be demanded by an adoptive family. He understood, if obscurely, that it might be less emotionally taxing to have someone who offered the tolerant understanding of acquaintanceship rather than the bonds of intimacy; Pennery he sensed would offer him more scope for personal development. Had he been older, or been questioned more closely, he might have explained that having, metaphorically, considered the possible options he had decided Pennery would regard him neither as a precious possession nor a burden. The Reverend Patterson, he intuited, would probably wish to make him Kip *Patterson* rather than Kip Harrison.

Also, in the far reaches of his mind lurked a vague suspicion that somehow he was to blame for what had happened and instinctively shied away from inviting further tragedy. Twice he had forged bonds of dependence and affection; first with his parents and then with his great aunt. Each time suddenly, inexplicably, the support and love he had come to cherish, to depend on, had been abruptly terminated. *If you loved someone too much, did you doom them?* He had loved his parents – they died: he had come to love his great aunt – she died. *Had he loved them less would they all still be alive?* It was perhaps the legacy of these tragic circumstances a subconscious combination of all these factors that led him to choose the companionship of the emotionally undemanding schoolmaster.

ii

On the Sunday afternoon of Kip's *defiant truancy* as Patterson put it in the rigidly disciplined thick black script on which he prided himself, condemning **the boy's unacceptable behaviour** which was **setting a very bad example.** He, Pennery, **was not doing his job as a guardian and if it was without your permission** (but probably with Pennery's acquiescence, or even encouragement, was implied) that Kip had **deliberately absented himself then at very least the boy deserves a good thrashing for his disobedience...** He concluded aggressively **You, Pennery are now in loco parentis! He is your ward! You have the privilege to be his guardian. He is in all respects now your son and as The Book has it, Whoever spareth the rod hateth his son but he who loves him is diligent to discipline him.**

This note was followed up the next day by a visit to the schoolhouse. Pennery explained that he did not see the offence, if indeed it was an offence, as a very serious one and that the boy had been most apologetic, surprised and embarrassed that his absence had been noticed. Pennery knew that when Kip's aunt had been alive they had rarely attended except at Christmas and Easter, and Patterson had raised no objection then. He wondered whether the Minister knew she had been heard to show impatience at Patterson's sermonising didacticism.

"It was evidently a spur-of-the-moment thing," Pennery offered mildly, "I'm sure it won't happen again." He had no intention whatever of punishing the boy and his refusal to be either annoyed or intimidated, left Patterson striking the air. A satisfactory dispute required two participants at least; shadow-boxing in anger is merely ludicrous. Patterson, recognising the situation, retired defeated although nobody else in Salter's Creek would have dreamed that there had been any question of 'victory' or 'defeat'. Pennery himself was unaware that there had been even the suggestion of a battle. The schoolmaster was not seen as a sad man, but rather as a man who kept everyone at arm's length. Something in his past which manifested itself in a certain reticence, led to people speculating on a bereavement or even, their imagination stimulated by increasing rumours that the heir to the English throne was liaising with a divorcee, the aftermath of a bitter divorce. Why else should he choose to bury himself in the fastness of Salter's Creek? His innate reticence prevented Salter's Creek appreciating that, having been tutored in a 'school' far harsher that any of them had experienced, or could ever imagine, he had had enough of being responsible for making decisions which affected the lives of others. Had Patterson ever suspected this it would have confirmed his inner conviction of Pennery's unsuitability as the boy's guardian.

Nonetheless, whatever the reasons, he and Patterson had skirmished ever since his arrival. Intellectually confident, Pennery saw no need to establish himself by indulging in small eccentricities as a lesser man might have felt impelled to do. Above all he had no wish to offend those he taught and liked. Unusually for a schoolmaster of that time and place, he respected his pupils as individuals, something which had probably impressed itself on Kip's subconscious.

Although it would never have occurred to Pennery deliberately to absent himself from church, he saw no particular merit in condemning the non-attendance of those who felt strongly against it for whatever reason. Despite the extreme sectarianism of the founding fathers and except for one or two families in the outlying settlements, Salter's Creek was not any longer fanatically religious. It was however jealous of its communal spirit, a relic of days when the mere fact that a community could exist at all in the midst of inhospitable wilderness was a source of pride. The small population was insufficient to support competitive enterprises of any sort. There was one church as there was one store and one shabby hotel; families went to church as much to keep in touch as anything. Salter's Creek had never quite matured into an *urban* community as Pennery, perhaps alone, recognised. If the township ever expanded then no doubt church attendance would fall away and, under the impact of larger numbers, the community would disintegrate into separate self-interested little groups – but that was in the future, if at all.

The schoolmaster was not an irreligious man although he upheld no particular dogma. For Pennery the existence of God was a fact, quite as much as it was for Leonard Patterson. However Patterson's God required man to travel through life according to an inflexible set of rules which, it seemed, were interpretable only by Patterson himself, whereas Pennery's Creator sat back watching with a curious, even amused objective eye to see whatever his Creation would get up to next – Success or Failure? Loyalty or Treachery? Kindness or Cruelty?

Although both Pennery and Patterson inherited and, more important, manifested in their personalities, something of their different conceptions of God, they would both have been shocked had it been suggested they merely deified one favoured part of their own very human natures. Pennery's God was personal and immediate, both understanding and unreliable: Patterson's remote but utterly dependable in his severity. Pennery attended church because he recognised that as the schoolmaster it was expected of him and he did so automatically, neutrally, without having to steel himself to the ordeal. There was, for him, no battle of wills, it was his Duty. Ironically his presence was sometimes interpreted by Patterson as provocation.

Pennery's tranquillity of mind was not laziness, rather it sprang from intellectual equilibrium. He assumed that there were two or more sides to every question; personal commitment was determined by balancing arguments for and against. He saw no reason to ensure those he taught had to commit themselves to his own point of view. Above all, he declined to assume responsibility for what others decided to do or say. Quite unsuspected by anyone in Salter's Creek, his whole philosophy of life could be summarised by the fact that not only did he rarely make decisions, but that he had at last found the peace which comes from having no decisions to make.

He was rarely engaged by Patterson's perorations. From an intellectual standpoint, he went into neutral, allowing his thoughts to wander away from the congregation sitting edgily in the uncomfortable pews; words flowed over and through him unacknowledged. Only the schoolmaster, of all those in Salter's Greek enduring the Sunday service, might have faulted the sermons on intellectual grounds. He could have refuted utterly the Minister's convoluted reasoning had he been so inclined but he seemed to harbour a secret intellectual inner weariness which was not lethargy. Patterson demonstrated too little coherent philosophy, too much dramatic rhetoric, too great a reliance on sheer oratory for Pennery; the Minister's arguments lacked the intellectual integrity to prompt the schoolmaster even to confront his own beliefs, let alone to rouse him enough to challenge Patterson's dogmatic and rigid theology.

Thus it was that Patterson's sermons offered Pennery time to relax. He could not read or write there in church – that would give offence – but there could be none given if he simply ceased to listen, for who should know? Paterson fumed in silence misinterpreting Pennery's apparent absorption as niggling concentration on his words from the very pulpit – *the schoolmaster was searching for faulty reasoning!* He might have been more annoyed still had he realised Pennery was not even listening, let alone bothering to muster any counter arguments. The Minister had to make sure that a side was taken and, furthermore, that the side taken should be what he *knew* to be the *correct* side. Pennery felt no strong partisanship even for his own ideas. Patterson would have interpreted this as evidence of a very weak mind without realising that, alternatively, it might be the sign of an exceptionally strong one. The Minister was a proselytizer, the schoolmaster a philosopher.

Perhaps Pennery's unique tranquillity during these Sunday mornings took him closer to God than ever Patterson came, although admittedly it would have been Pennery's God. Had Pennery's deity been recognised by Patterson it would have approximated more closely to the Minister's conception of the devil. Pennery did not care who else believed in his God or his Devil; Patterson cared passionately because he believed, with an arrogance which he never acknowledged he possessed, that his own God was *The One and Only God*. He, Patterson *knew* that *anything* else was, by definition, *Evil* and must be destroyed. It was his mission in life to make everyone agree with him.

The Minister was at heart a man of faction and, faction being absent from his life, it was something he unconsciously missed. Had Pennery actually belittled him, Patterson would have resented the fact. Nonetheless at the same time he would have welcomed such a response as a call to arms. Open hostility would inevitably have divided the community; his supporters would have rallied with the unquestioning loyalty which even a bad general inspires on the eve of battle, in which case Patterson divined, a degree of martyrdom would have invested him. But the Minister was no fool. In his wiser moments Patterson admitted to himself that by the very fact of human nature, one section of public opinion would have supported Pennery and however much he would have delighted in a battle, he realised that to take the offensive without any obviously justifiable cause would merely make matters worse. The schoolmaster seemed, somehow, a more sympathetic character than himself, a man who might well inspire the greater measure of support were *he* to be seen as the victim in which case Pennery might even become the martyr instead.

Intuitively aware, if only dimly, that Pennery could, if he chose, destroy his own rigid theology, Patterson, in his more optimistic moments, interpreted the schoolmaster's presence in church as a victory for everything that he and the Sunday service stood for. To a certain extent he may have been right, for public opinion, if consulted, might have agreed that it subscribed largely to Patterson's version of God and, as a complement to this, it expected Pennery to be present every Sunday just as surely as if the matter had been one of the terms written into his teaching contract. Sometimes however, when uncomfortable flashes of insight intruded even as he preached, Patterson knew that his argument was specious and interpreted the schoolmaster's mere presence as deliberate provocation. At these, and similar moments, he would have been delighted had Pennery refused, publically, to attend church. It would have constituted a justifiable *casus belli*, an unmistakable sign that the schoolmaster was deliberately defying Patterson and all that Patterson stood for: a declaration of war which would justify him mustering the full force of conventional opinion behind him. Ironically enough, in reading Pennery's presence either as his own victory, or as deliberate provocation, Patterson was utterly mistaken. He accorded to Pennery motives which were never present.

They had fenced with each other for years. Occasionally at a meeting Pennery took conversational advantage or, over some unimportant matter, made a debating point because he felt that Patterson expected it of him. He knew that his own foil was buttoned and attributed similar lack of malice to the Minister; Patterson's sallies against Pennery were made with the intention of wounding.

Rarely however did any of this ruffle the surface of life in Salter's Creek. If Patterson possessed human failings, he also possessed human virtues. He liked to help those in trouble, though a certain shyness, stemming from a desire never to exhibit emotion or, worse, sentimentality, frequently led him to provide more logical, though less endearing, reasons for his reactions.

The difference between them could be summarised by their instinctive attitude to Pope Potter had they been asked. Patterson would have confidently asserted the old man's madness resulted from his apparent inability to determine precisely what was Divine and what Satanic: Pennery would have suggested that perhaps it was exactly this tormenting uncertainty which showed Pope Potter to be saner than the rest of them.

5

i

Patterson preached well enough, even Loxton would have admitted that. If sermons *had* to be preached at all, then Salter's Creek supposed Patterson did as good a job as was possible. There was no personal resentment of the Minister, that was reserved for the content of the sermons alone; it was merely an unpopular aspect of an otherwise respectable job. By tacit understanding, sermons were classified in the same category as Loxton's decisions, announced in bold broad-banded panels of *The Sentinel* that the **further rise in the school rate was a most regrettable communal necessity**. This generosity of spirit led people to assume it was the office Patterson held, rather than the man who held it, that was responsible for the imposition, of the ritual Sunday sermon.

It occurred to nobody except occasionally Pennery and, in the past the late Miss Harrison, to enquire into the reasons for Patterson saying some of the things he did. Perhaps, had it been asked to account for the Minister's sentiments, Salter's Creek would have said that it supposed he received a package each week from the church superiors. Inside the package there would of course be the sermon of the day, or at least the subject for the sermon of the day. People assumed that his church was there to prevent them from doing the things they really wanted to do but which they knew were not really respectable. Patterson, as the current incumbent, was bound to point out error; he had, as it were, a direct line from a God, who apparently viewed the world as a whole, and Salter's Creak in particular, with a somewhat jaundiced eye.

Because of this unfocused, illogical yet amiable attitude, Salter's Creek pardoned Patterson when he sounded particularly Calvinistic or when he expressed a particularly uncomfortable view with dogmatic virulence. Patterson himself took full advantage of this good-natured tolerance. It enabled him to express his inner conviction without suffering the social embarrassment which some of his pronouncements from the pulpit might have otherwise occasioned.

The Minister was wracked by dilemmas of his own making. Had he lived at an earlier age he would have made the perfect martyr: the pillar of the Stylites, the hermitage of St Jerome in the Wilderness would have been his chosen residence. Due to enter a lion-inhabited arena and having prepared himself for a dreadful death, he would have wept, not at the prospect of pain, but at the possibility of deliverance. These facets of his personality might have alarmed him had he ever allowed himself to be conscious of them, the essence of an asceticism that he never fully recognised. None of this however was evident to those who met him and talked with him as their Minister.

He sometimes wondered whether his congregation felt that he had failed to set an example. Was his failure to have a 'proper family' a social betrayal of Salter's Creek, as well as the sexual betrayal of his wife? He saw no way of explaining satisfactorily either to himself or his wife why and how his deep spiritual obligation to his God took precedence over his biological obligation to her and setting an example to the community. It was a sign of Patterson's utter self-absorption that he never realised Salter's Creek never blamed him for lack of family; they understood that sometimes even the most loving couples were denied children.

Until his marriage Patterson had been a man filled with the confidence that he was always in control himself. Discovering the overpowering drive of his more animal nature shocked him profoundly. Before the honeymoon he had never suspected how deep were the roots of his sexual desire; he had regarded himself as a man who was in complete control of everything except his Soul – which he allowed to God. When the ecstasy of sexual congress (and it *was* ecstasy) had exhausted itself and relaxation flowed back into his consciousness, Patterson became increasingly aware of his total lack of control over his lust.

If it had worried him the first time it occurred, his inner conflict had developed into ever-present agony of spirit when it continued ever more urgently as night followed night. Anticipation of their love-making dominated his daytime thoughts as much as its fulfilment filled his nights. Had he been a more courageous man, he might have changed, become more humble, recognised that for all his theology he too was no more than sensual animal. Instead he decided that he should not endanger his spiritual nature further. Having forced himself to admit there was a decision to be made he was unable to rest until he had committed himself utterly.

He was no prude; the physical act of love-making, which he sincerely believed were permissible to Man, did not disgust him. To begin with none of this was inconsistent with his clerical functions and marriage vows. What took him by surprise was discovering his uninhibited enjoyment of erogenous contact, the subtle pressures of flesh on flesh. It was the *urgency* of desire love-making unleashed that terrified him. It seemed to be a force so primitive, so seductive, that it *must* be pagan for it nullified in an instant every intellectual reservation that he had expected would have restrained the engulfing passion of sexual congress with his lawful spouse. He feared it might – no, more than that – he *knew* it would become overwhelmingly necessary to him. He had trained himself to disbelieve and, above all, to distrust emotion, yet at this crisis he suspected that even within him, Leonard Patterson, there lurked dark, even Satanic, impulses which cast Reason to the wind and surrendered him to a destructive emotional turmoil both passionate and intense. It seemed as though his God had betrayed him or, rather, that *he* had betrayed his God.

For those few fearful months he fought the battle internally, traumatised by a sense of sinfulness at being so easily decoyed from his self-imposed stoicism. Eventually there came the moment when, overcome by nausea at his own perfidy, he vomited in the bathroom retching out, as it were, the loathsome animality that still clung to him. Then he had bathed, scrubbing his body all over hard and hurtfully. Before the sun rose, he had made the irrevocable decision, total celibacy.

He did not tell his wife, nor could he admit even to himself that, although innate masculinity accepted and rejoiced in procreation, his intellectual arrogance rebelled at the degree of emotional involvement which lay bound-up with it. Had he been drawn less powerfully to the sexual satisfaction he found with his wife, he might have been as pleased and willing to couple with her in the necessary act of procreation as he would to wash his face or eat a good dinner. He hoped desperately that those decadent nights, as he now thought of them, would prove fruitful, prayed that his wife was pregnant. Days passed, then weeks, until it was obvious that there would be no child. His prayers had gone unheard; it was a judgment on him.

He accustomed himself, at first over months and then years, to accept that lack of children was to be the cross he had to bear throughout life; childlessness was a Divine punishment, denial of their united bodies was the appropriate sacrifice demanded by a disapproving God. At the time he gave little consideration to the possibility that he might be sacrificing his wife as well. It never occurred to him that the depth of the passion he discovered in his sexuality might be a firmer guarantee of a loving God than all the theological arguments in his library. Had it been suggested to him that it was perhaps at precisely those moments he was closest to God, he would have condemned it as blasphemous.

It was very largely sympathy for what he interpreted as his wife's longing for children which had provoked Patterson into suggesting that Kip Harrison should live with them. He did not himself really understand children, but his wife had always wanted children, one at very least. Moreover as the religious leader of the community it was after all up to him to set an example. If it was his sense of duty both as husband *and* Minister which persuaded him to make the offer to adopt the boy, what filled him with secret exultation was belief that it was a sign of forgiveness: by providing a child for his wife to mother, God had at last pardoned his Minister's one-time lust.

He was not without sympathy for the boy and somebody had to be prepared to house, feed and guide him. Furthermore what little he had seen of Kip had impressed him. Not only was he a good-looking child, but he seemed biddable and polite: a son old enough to be a credit to them while still young and tractable enough to disturb the tenor of their life very little. Patterson's sympathy was however extended in a formal way, lacking any warm personal touch: a child without parents or home was, *de facto*, an object of pity, worthy of sympathy, that was an inevitable extension of his conception of religion. Whether the boy was Kip Harrison in Salter's Creek or an Indian orphan thousands of miles away made no difference to the 'right' response.

Every child deserved to be loved; it was their right. In Patterson's philosophy it was an archetypal situation and he had reacted with commendable sincerity in the accepted manner it demanded. The boy needed guidance, care and affection. The snag was that Patterson had no conception of what 'affection' truly demanded, or what 'love' involved. Even more unfortunate was the fact that he was blissfully unaware of his ignorance. 'Love' for Patterson was something which his interpretation of religion taught him to take for granted; it existing instantly between husband and wife from the moment they exchanged marriage vows, conferred by virtue of the terminology.

'Love' restored order to chaos; it was something convenient and placid which brought refinement into a life which might otherwise be merely a savage emotional jungle. Furthermore he equated 'love' with 'respect'; as a child he had as a matter of course respected his own father and respect implied obedience. The possibility that he himself had never 'loved' his parents (nor for that matter, anyone else) having never occurred to him, he was secure in his delusions. That all children and all parents loved each other was a fact of life, therefore every adopted child and its adoptive parents would instantly assume the same relationship: parents died, children wept and then their appointed guardians would be equally loved, respected and obeyed. It never occurred to Patterson, who was not a dishonest man, that love had to flow both ways, that it might be a strong, subtle, evolving bond capable of an infinite variety of adjustments, of moods, of kindnesses and disappointments. His obtuseness stemmed basically from his deep-rooted distrust of emotion: 'love' for Patterson was a species of limpet which, prized from one surface, attached itself immediately and just as firmly to another.

In the last analysis it would have been inaccurate to assume that Patterson's decision to offer Kip a home contained no trace of another very human motive which had stolen up on him unexpectedly; the realisation that he required a son. Patterson was not without the inborn vanity of most men: he needed a son to act as a memorial to him when he was dead. It was a notion he had never previously considered but which now seemed a necessary adjunct to the sort of man he wanted the community to respect as their pastor: a son was the corollary to everything that he had become. However, to do him justice, this instinct, refined and controlled as it had been hitherto, was the least consideration in his reasoning when he had initially offered to adopt the boy.

Kip's rejection of his offer came as a stunning blow. Quite unjustifiably he had concluded that the boy's decision to spurn his offer to adopt him had been due to Pennery's malign advice. Pennery's refusal to punish the boy for absenting himself from church confirmed his suspicions; the schoolmaster had at very least turned a blind eye...*even deliberately encouraged the boy to stay away from church*? It served further to exacerbate Patterson's hostility towards the schoolmaster.

ii

Had anyone in Salter's Creek been asked for an example of an ideal marriage they would, without hesitation, have nominated the Pattersons. Joyce Patterson they knew would have been a caring mother, lack of children was merely a matter of bad luck, the way things happened even to the most deserving.

At the beginning, when her husband had taken her with unexpected, fierceness, she was filled first with alarm, then wonder, and finally with delight. Those times stayed in her memory as paradisiacal. Then things had begun to change. Now, when she looked back regretfully on the early days of their marriage as increasingly she did, she brooded.

That unforgettable night she had woken to find her husband no longer by her side, unaware that he had been similarly absent from their bed the two previous nights. In the light patch of the window, she had seen him, still as a statue, outlined against a dawn sky, hands clasped as if in prayer. Instinctively, she guessed that his unease was something to do with both of them. It was after this she acknowledged to herself that there had been a distinct falling off in their physical intimacy. Eventually they ceased to share the same bed; now, at Salter's Creek, they had separate rooms.

Joyce Patterson was essentially a woman with an infinite capacity for being happy but she could make herself equally miserable when she was worried. She did not, and could not, guess at the streak of asceticism which invested Leonard Patterson's soul. She understood only that he had abandoned the intimacy of married life, but she did not know why and therefore sought an explanation.

She was not an unintelligent woman, nor was she ignorant and slowly, over a period of time, she believed she had deduced the underlying reason. Her deductions were logical – logical that was to say, in the light of those aspects of her husband's behaviour that she noticed. Her mistake was compounded by the fact that, as time when on, she noticed only things which tended to support her reluctant conclusion. It never occurred to her that her husband rode his emotions and desires as a novice rides a spirited horse, afraid that his mount, beyond his control, might run away with him. Had she realised this, or had she been bolder, she might have made efforts to win him back. At that early stage it would have been easy. She was however too timid. Eventually she found herself left with only one possible explanation: Leonard was not fond of women. Months passed, the notion hardened and led her to another supposition. Perhaps, all along she had been afraid of this for, once the idea took old on her imagination, it became a certainty.

Aged five she had not been allowed to attend her father's funeral. For years she remembered him only as a somewhat distant figure in the warm old vicarage; a busy house, with a constant stream of parish visitors, especially village children bigger and older than her, choirboys, Cubs, Scouts. Some of them would stop to push her on the swing which hung from the great horse-chestnut tree. She remembered very vividly the desolation of packing up; empty rooms, curtain-less windows. Then her grandmother's grey pile in a grim northern industrial town loomed over by grime-windowed mills and tall chimneys belching smoke that choked damp narrow cobbled streets. In her imagination the sun never shone there.

The old lady, gaunt and domineering as the streets and chimneys, referred openly to her grand-daughter as 'her mother's little burden' even, occasionally, as 'another mistake', her father never mentioned except in whispered conversations.

She had been glad when she and her mother boarded the great liner to Canada, remembered with gratitude their warm reception by the remote but kindly Episcopalian bishop in Toronto to whom her mother now became housekeeper; he had been a close friend of her father when they were both young ordinands in England. Gradually the sun came out again and continued to shine until, not long married, clearing her mother's rooms after her death, she came across part of a newspaper cutting, brown with age slipped between the sheets of a blotting folder:

SUICIDE VICAR'S SECRET VICE

Yesterday Nauntwich Coroner concluded that Reverend Thomas Milven had taken his own life while the balance of his mind was disturbed.

He was awaiting sentence having pleaded guilty to inappropriate behaviour, indecency and gross indecency with boys aged from eight to thirteen.

The offences occurred over a period of fifteen years whilst he was Vicar of the rural parish of St Swithin's in the picturesque Naunton Ferrar, one of England's prettiest villages which feature in all the guides because each August, uniquely for a Church of England parish, it commemorates the Catholic martyr, Margaret Clitherow ('The Pearl of York') who in 1586

Which boys? Those who had played with her, joked, pushed her on the swing? Suddenly, the memory she had for so long successfully repressed came back to her as shocking and vividly as if had been yesterday: between two dark-suited men, her father walking away down the flower-bordered path without even a backward glance to her and her mother standing in the rose-clustered porch. None of this had she ever mentioned to Patterson. He knew her only as the self-sufficient eighteen-year-old girl who had taken on her elderly mother's housekeeping duties for the frail octogenarian Bishop to whom he had been Chaplain and who had married them with his blessing only months before he died peacefully in his sleep.

From the moment she found the cutting she had ceased to look rationally at Leonard Patterson's behaviour; newspaper reports of similar scandals in distant places seemed to force themselves on her attention with uncanny regularity until 'clergyman' and 'indecent behaviour' became synonymous in her mind.

Although there was not one fragment of truth in her supposition, such was her delusion that trivial occasions involving children (part and parcel of his everyday parochial duties) assumed increasingly sinister implications. Had she even hinted at her suspicions to anyone in Salter's Creek they would have listened in amazed disagreement, wondering if perhaps she was in some way unwell. Leonard Patterson was not homosexual (the idea repelled him) let alone a pederast. He was one of those rare, truly virginal, individuals who, had he lived a thousand years earlier would have been revered as a holy recluse. His great misfortune was that although his true vocation was that of a hermit, he'd been born into to a time and a world which no longer believed in saints.

Because she was a sensitive woman and because she had loved her husband unconditionally from the moment they first met, she decided that his 'difficulty' (as she chose to think of it) was something they must now live with, she determined to be a saviour and source of strength to her husband. Although there remained coruscating fear that he might compromise himself utterly, her love for him was, at that early stage, too deep for her to harbour any suspicion that he might even prefer Kip to herself.

The now ineradicable memory of that final time she had glimpsed her own father's humiliating departure dictated the perspective through which she continued to view the present: only her constant vigilance could save her husband. When, in the course of congregational duties he had gone to talk to the Scouts, to a Boys' Club, visit a school, she felt a shiver of apprehension. Although she never knew date, time or duration of the girls' Confirmation class, she knew to the minute the time the boys' class was due to end and if Patterson were unexpectedly delayed she sweated with fearful love. As years passed her fear-fuelled imagination crystallized entirely innocuous incidents into seemingly damning facts, but she lacked the courage to broach the topic with him.

If their eventual move from busy city parish to the remoteness of Salter's Creek brought Patterson as close as he would ever get to the solitariness his instincts sought, for her it came as a blessed relief, removing him from an urban environment where, in her own fevered imagination, situations arose which must tempt him constantly.

Nevertheless, even at Salter's Creek, whenever she saw him talking to one of the boys who came from an outlying homestead a pang of cold dread went through her, certain it preceded his fall from grace. Convinced her husband was being kept under observation, she was particularly reluctant to entertain Dill Randall and his wife.

When Patterson told her he had offered to become the boy's guardian, to take Kip Harrison into their home, she felt quite numb. Like a stroke. For a long minute she could hardly speak. It confirmed utterly what, in her few rare optimistic moments, she had striven to dismiss as unfounded imagination on her part. For an hour after he had told her she suffered a state of shock. Patterson was stunned by her reaction which he misinterpreted. He had not, he reasoned to himself, realised how passionately she had wanted a child and that now, having given up all hope for so long, she was too overcome with happiness to take in the good news.

He blamed himself for his blindness. Never much interested in having a family (though now the thought of a foster-son, seemed suddenly entirely appropriate) he admitted his selfishness: he had never sympathetically considered *her* longing for a child. He should have suggested adoption years earlier; there had been plenty of opportunity in the city parish which he had ministered for a decade.

Gradually Joyce Patterson pulled herself back to normality and, by the time they were drinking a cup of tea together in the late afternoon, it had occurred to her that there might be something advantageous in the situation. If they adopted the boy, she persuaded herself Leonard's interest in him would appear quite proper to the outside world. The boy would think nothing untoward in her husband's 'fondness' for him were he, in effect, the boy's step-father – as he would be if they formally adopted him. In the furthest recesses of her mind there were also half-evolved notions which she dared not allow to crystallise.

Timid as she was, there lay in Joyce Patterson an unsuspected steeliness, a streak of ruthlessness roused by fear for the reputation of her husband. If Leonard were as infatuated as she had convinced herself he was, then to have the boy living in their house, dependent on them as he would be, he would be reluctant to complain should any unfortunate incident occur despite her vigilance. She would have been shocked into horrified denial had it been put to her in so many words, but nevertheless, underlying her attitude lurked an unpalatable fact that she refused to confront: Joyce Patterson was prepared to accept young Kip Harrison's presence in the house as providing a sort of safety valve. In recognising and accepting her husband's 'difficulty', Joyce Patterson was determined to protect him from the consequences at all costs: if it came to a choice between public disgrace for her husband and an occasional undesirable experience for the boy, she had no compunction as to the choice she would make.

In this way, in the darkest cavities of her mind, was sown the seed of an immorality so shocking that nobody except perhaps Pennery would have been able to appreciate its magnitude. Although the insidiousness of her self-corruption had begun to nibble her conscience, even as she sought to assure herself that she was justified in her attitude, she failed to perceive the depths of the moral abyss before her. Had she done so she might have embraced the safety of madness long before she actually did. Furthermore, had life at Salter's Creek not left its familiar undramatic groove then it is doubtful whether Joyce Patterson's essential immorality or her husband's inflexible pride would have mattered at all.

News of Kip's refusal had shocked her too. After the initial moment of sheer relief that he would *not* be coming to tempt her husband another, darker, suspicion rode her even more fiercely. *Why had the boy refused?* It could only be because Leonard had already molested or attempted to molest him and these unwelcome 'advances' had frightened him off.

Throughout the days which followed she waited dark-eyed, dreading the telephone's ring, the arrival of an official letter, an unannounced visit from Randall. It never occurred to her that Loxton would do other than make the boy give good reasons for his refusal of the Pattersons' offer. In her tortured mind she imagined conspiracy – secret conferences behind closed doors, drawn curtains, surreptitious looks of censure, whispered conversations – where none existed. Pennery was the arm of retribution: the boy had certainly told *him* about Leonard and Pennery would have told Randall, if Loxton had not already done so. Was there any explanation other than the one she had conjured-up? *Could it be that her husband was jealous of Pennery's 'association' with the boy?* What if his envy should lead him to force the issue into the open thus convicting himself as the sordid truth emerged – was he preparing her for the blow that might fall at any moment?

His wife's strained face and continued nervousness worried Patterson. He put it down to her disappointment after setting her heart on mothering the boy. Her reaction was further justification for disliking Pennery. He sought to comfort her with what he intended to be reassuring comments…"Kip's refusal is of course due to that Pennery's influence"…"What boys of that age really need is a Christian family"…"Loving care of a mother"…"Affectionate but disciplinary guidance of a father"… totally unaware that they merely confirmed his wife's bizarre conviction that he was excusing his own unsavoury conduct.

It was perhaps the ultimate irony that, even if Joyce Patterson had been correct in her misinterpretation of her husband's motives and inclinations, she would have had nothing to fear. There was no way she could have guessed that it would never occur to Kip Harrison to make any complaint. Too immature to be sexually aware, he would have been neither deeply disturbed nor guiltily aroused as he might have been had he been a year or two older. He might have been bored, even innocently co-operative but not surprised that anyone should wish to behave in that way. It would have been just one more of the bizarre expectations of the mystifying alien adult world into which he had been thrust. After all hadn't they too been well-meaning adults – those who'd expected him to *enjoy* slimy boiled tripe and tapioca pudding during his hospitalised convalescence before his great aunt rescued him? Furthermore why should it matter to anyone else what happened to him? He had *mattered* first to his parents, then to his aunt and look what had happened to them? He, Kip Harrison, was a danger to anyone who bothered themselves too much about *him*, which was why he had instinctively chosen an emotionally uncommitted companionship which would endanger nobody.

The decision that the boy should go and live with somebody else had come as a huge relief to Joyce Patterson. However, it had taken a long time before she had managed, if not to dispel fears about her husband's predilection but, at the very least, to come to terms with his 'difficulties' and she had only just begun to sleep easily again. It was therefore particularly unfortunate that the boy's absence from church revived allegations, first made at the time of the Smokers Club affair, which suggested Pennery was far too lenient to remain Kip's guardian and the boy might come to them after all.

6

SMOKERS CLUB SCANDAL *The Sentinel* headline had screamed almost exactly three years earlier during a similarly long dry spell shortly after Kip had arrived in the community. A few drops of rain had fallen on the thirteenth of June but that was the end of it. Randall had become increasingly worried about fire risk. There had already been three small fires occasioned by travellers stopping to brew up on the verge deep in pine needles scuffed up by passing vehicles on the hazardous-to-tyres loose surface of the narrow through-way. Anxiety had been heightened by one particular blaze deeper in the forest which had started nobody knew how. Each spring he personally ensured that the fire-watching platform at Three Pines Rough was thoroughly checked and renovated after winter snow and strong gales. Later in the year, or much earlier, in the winter for instance when the forest was not creaking with dryness and snow was prevalent, the Smokers Club affair would not have aroused the hysteria it did, but that spring had been as rainless as the current summer now promised to be and remembrance of forest fires in the past put everyone on edge.

'Timber' McKay was the grandson of one of the earliest and certainly dourest settlers whose father had spent his early childhood with impoverished relations in Glasgow until his parents had scraped enough together to pay for his passage to join them. He had discovered Calum, his ten-year-old son, had been in the habit of smoking. He complained furiously to Loxton on a crackling telephone line that "before gie'in' him a beltin' on his backside he'll no ferget", he had learned that illicit smoking was a regular after-school activity indulged in by 'The Smokers Club' which was "a verra close-guarded secret". It had come to light when his wife, dominated by her husband and much embittered by the struggle to keep food on the table for a family of six, found a half-smoked cigarette in his son's pocket. "It's all the fault of yon dominie," he spat. "Discipline at the school, is aye slack to say the verra least! That Pennery is a weak disciplinarian. Those of us," McKay fulminated, "who learned our book under Auld Belter (the legendary and much feared 'dominie' of his boyhood) rarely went a week wi'oot gaein' hame wi' a verra sore aarrse!"

Pennery who had no inkling such a 'Club' existed, had investigated. It turned out that the 'it consisted of a fluid group who filched cigarettes from elder brothers and parents, then surreptitiously sneaked into the forest to share and smoke them on the way home from school. Although only about a dozen owned up, or were denounced by those who had confessed, Pennery had a suspicion that in fact most boys had participated at one time or another.

He left them in no doubt as to the sheer stupidity of their behaviour and it was his evident disappointment in their thoughtlessness which carried most weight for they respected, even liked him. He personally accepted the word of each of them individually that such hazardous idiocy should stop there and then. Kip, then just in his first months at Salter's Creek, admitted that he had been present on one occasion some weeks earlier, by accident rather than intention. Invited to join the others when they set off to the enticingly named Splash-Puddle, he had done so under the mistaken impression they were going there to bathe. Pennery had found Kip refreshingly truthful; he accepted entirely the boy's assurance that he had himself never actually smoked.

Nevertheless it had seemed, even to Randall, that Pennery's measures were half-hearted. "Shouldn't you have thrashed them all? They won't appreciate the seriousness of carelessly dropping matches or half-smoked cigarettes in the undergrowth unless a great deal more fuss is made and the best way to achieve that is for them to find they can't sit down comfortably for a week! Those remote forest clearings, particularly inaccessible, thick with dry brambles, are an exceptionally high fire risk even at the wettest of times."

Pennery resisted the temptation to point out that it had taken place outside the school, well after school hours and was not therefore a matter for school discipline. Instead he explained patiently that not only had the boys ensured they smoked in a place where they were unlikely to be seen but, conscious of fire risk, they'd enough sense to choose Splash-Puddle, the one place where there was least chance of an accidental fire. Crystal-clear water from a spring in the rock filled a wide sandy-bottomed pool before disappearing down another fissure as unexpected as the first. Pennery, in his famous lecture, had explained it as a faulting of harder rock in surrounding limestone, worn smooth during the geological past by the constant flow of water *"and perhaps more recently"* he had added with a laugh, *"by the pad of bare feet"*. It was a popular bathing place, quite deep enough for younger and smaller children to swim a few strokes.

Nevertheless he had made quite clear the foolishness of their behaviour and of the disastrous consequences even dropping a match could have on their homes, They were, he had emphasised, now terrified, not of being beaten again (as most of them already had been by their fathers) but by having been forced to confront the disastrous consequences of carelessly cast-down cigarette butts. He was, he emphasised, quite certain the Smokers Club was a thing of the past.

Later he began to wonder whether he had gone too far in his depiction of the consequences their behaviour could have on their homes when two of the leaders, hollow-eyed and genuinely frightened, came separately and privately to seek his advice because they were suffering from harrowing nightmares in which fire roared through the forest engulfing them and their families.

Instead of tackling Pennery to his face, McKay wrote to *The Sentinel.* This was perhaps understandable; the McKays lived deep in the forest where the fallen needles and even the trees themselves were so dry that any fire, however small and accidental, threatened disaster, but his pithy letter had unforeseen consequences.

Although Randall had, by the following morning, accepted the schoolmaster's observation that for the youngsters to choose Splash-Puddle showed considerable common sense (far more in fact than passing motorists who boiled up kettles by the roadside!) they had parted that afternoon on terms which, if not positively acrimonious, were certainly cool. It was therefore particularly unfortunate that the same evening, still irritated by Pennery's reasoned advocacy on behalf of the culprits, he had been overheard in casual conversation wondering aloud whether the schoolmaster's apparent leniency "should be deplored rather than admired" which was subsequently interpreted by the uncharitable as 'official' endorsement of McKay's splenetic letter in *The Sentinel.*

This in turn prompted Patterson to raise Pennery's 'disgraceful civic leniency' as he chose to phrase it, from the pulpit the following Sunday morning. "*Where* had the Smokers Club had formed itself however clandestinely? *At Our School.*" It merited "the severest *school* punishment. *All* the culprits deserved to have been soundly thrashed *by the schoolmaster,*" thundered Patterson. "With *no* exceptions! '**The rod and reproof give wisdom…but a child left to himself brings shame to his mother and father…Folly is bound up in the heart of the child but the rod of discipline drives it far from him!**' *Proverbs,* **twenty-nine!**" With an audible slap of the pages, he slammed closed the great Bible on the lectern in front of him.

The Salters Creek Crier & Sentinel, traditionally referred to as *The Sentinel*, was owned, written and edited by Enoch Maguire. He had been left it by the distant uncle who had emigrated and after whom he had been named. He came all the way from the north of Ireland to inherit what he imagined to be a prosperous publishing house only to discover that it was a rural newspaper with one reporter, one typesetter and a balance of almost fifty dollars. Unable to afford the fare back, Maguire stayed. The reporter drank himself into a virtually permanent stupor and the typesetter died soon afterwards. Unable to afford replacements, Maguire himself became Editor, Chief Reporter and Typesetter.

He was the settlement's sole Roman Catholic, a matter of some awe with children from strict Presbyterian families in one or two of the outlying farmsteads who half-expected to see him fly off on a broomstick. However the nearest priest was over eighty miles away and, apart from attending Christmas Mass during his first two years at Salter's Creek, Maguire had lapsed. He never permitted religious argument in the paper and made a point of his non-conformity by working ostentatiously on Sunday. For reasons which once had been medical, but became economical, Maguire neither smoked nor drank. He rarely attended social functions, spending any spare time mounting his magnificent collection of moths which he used to catch at night after he had seen the paper safely off the press. He was probably the only man in the wider community who had never heard Patterson preach, although he was always well informed by others about the content of the Sunday sermon which often provided topics for comment in his editorials.

He had made a success of *The Sentinel* just as he would have made a success of much larger newspapers, because he was a born newspaper man. He had the knack of interpreting the exact mood of the community before the men and women of Salter's Creek recognised they had a special mood to be interpreted. Even more important, he possessed an almost uncanny sense of timing. He seemed to know exactly the right moment to publish a letter, or an article, to write a leader or to kill a subject dead.

Every issue of *The Sentinel* sold out. Although by this time he could well-afford to pay both a full-time reporter and a typesetter, he employed no other staff except for 'Snapper' Williams, a lone eccentric who acted as occasional press photographer when he was not spending early-morning hours patiently recording birds and forest wildlife for magazines worldwide. It is probable that Maguire was now by far the wealthiest member of the community, but it was a measure of his self-effacement that nobody would have thought to suggest it. Furthermore his unsociability obscured him; like Pennery, but for entirely different reasons, he too was never addressed by his Christian name.

Perhaps his greatest achievement was that nobody ever attributed any controversial statement published in the paper to Maguire himself; he remained journalistically invisible, it was always *The Sentinel* which spoke and thus the pronouncements of the newspaper were accorded almost magisterial respect. If it acted as the voice of Salter's Creek, it was also accepted by the community as its conscience: *The Sentinel* had become the Salter's Creek's oracle, Maguire merely an acolyte at the shrine.

Until the Smokers Club revelations, the topic which had most concerned its readers as the season grew hotter and dryer had been danger of fire, particularly the readiness of their fire-fighting facilities. The fierce controversy following publication of McKay's letter encouraged a number of other community problems to be aired whether or not they had any obvious relevance: desirability (or not) of allowing boys to remain at school after they had reached the age of fourteen, lack of moral fibre in the younger generation, whether the community was really getting value for money as regards the 'Rate' imposed *"chiefly in order to comply with the Nationally increased salary for schoolmasters"* as one correspondent put it.

Passages from Patterson's sermon, particularly his quotations from Proverbs, subsequently cited in *The Sentinel* were complemented by a stinging editorial which served only to stir the pot: **The criminal thoughtlessness of young hooligans who literally played with fire thus endangering the entire community** was, it implied, due to the schoolmaster's failure to discipline his pupils.

Initially, Pennery's refusal to beat them had been regarded by the boys themselves as a sort of divine mercy; even those who had already been punished at home showed nothing more than wry envy at the luck of those whose parents were initially reluctant to be swayed by what others said or thought. However, although Pennery never mentioned them, the names of all those involved became widely known. It was a secret that could not be kept in that community scattered though it was and most parents were anxious to demonstrate that they too had the well-being of their tinder-dry environment at heart. The actual intentions of the boys and other subtler rights and wrongs of the matter did not come into their thinking for they, like their neighbours, had to wrench a living from the unrelenting terrain surrounding Salter's Creek. The upshot was that, after *The*

Sentinel 'had spoken', even formerly reluctant parents decided to follow McKay's example and apply strap, stick or hand with varying degrees of severity. At the same time a faint resentment engendered by the sermon and the editorial, allowed the more squeamish to imply that they reluctantly undertook a duty which Pennery had shirked.

Nevertheless the whole affair was little more than a nine-days-wonder and when there was no further editorial mention of the matter, Maguire having correctly interpreted a slight change of mood, the more thoughtful began to admit to themselves that perhaps they had allowed what was after all a boyish lark to loom disproportionately large.

Pennery took no further action regarding Kip's 'truancy' from church. Had it ever occurred to him to have second thoughts, *The Sentinel* editorial echoing Patterson's ranting sermon would merely have confirmed him in his mildness. In fact he had not read the paper until late on the Tuesday when his attention was drawn to it by the elder Miss Parroty when she came to house-keep, as she did every other day. As far as he was concerned the matter was closed. He regretted the publicity because, as he told Randall when the fuss had abated, he "had not seen that it helped anyone to have a dozen little boys going about with woebegone faces and sore bottoms. In fact," he'd said pointedly, "one or two of my pupils were cruelly, indeed savagely, beaten by parents who ought to know better."

Thus it was that the Minister's insistence that Kip's Sunday 'truancy' was due to his guardian's irresponsibility revived hazy memories of 'The Smokers Club Scandal' three years earlier, details of which had become blurred with the passage of time. Had not that too had been the result of schoolmaster disciplinary laxity? Unfortunately the Minister's condemnation together with

Pennery's apparent reluctance to adopt Kip officially began to nudge Loxton into questioning the wisdom of appointing him to look after the boy. Might the Pattersons be more suitable guardians after all?

The next time Loxton noticed the boy passing, he called him across, "I just wondered how you were getting on with Mr Pennery?"

"It's fine, Mr Loxton."

Loxton, having reflected on Patterson's implication that maybe they should review the question of Kip's guardianship, ventured, lightly, "You sure? I don't know I'd have been wanting to stay with my schoolmaster when I was your age."

Kip was silent for a moment. "He's not really like a teacher… even when he's teaching us. He's…well, just nice. An' he was in the war. My aunt told me he'd got a medal."

"Oh, what for?"

"When I asked him the other day he said…" screwing up his eyes trying to recall Pennery's words *"in war, medals come up with the rations…an…an soldiers prefer the rations."*

Had Loxton questioned him further Kip might have told him that the topic had arisen when he'd asked Pennery about three medals he'd found in a drawer in the desk he'd been told to use, totally unaware of both the significance of the letters after the name, let alone the implication of the hospital for treating shell-shocked officers to which the official-looking brown envelope into which they had been stuffed had been sent.

Capt./Acting Major J. Pennery-Fraser VC, DSO, MC, Craiglockhart War Hospital Edinburgh

"That's fine. Just wanted to make sure you were OK."

"I've got my own room upstairs, under the roof…. An' my things from my great aunt's house." Then, after another pause,

"Thing is…he doesn't *fuss*…he doesn't tell me what to *do*, you know. Some of the others say they are always being told what to do by their fathers, or uncles. Mr Pennery…well he sort of expects me to know…it's better that way."

"That's just dandy. As long as you're…OK." There was no doubt that the boy seemed happy enough and tanned by the sun he looked well cared for although he was still on the small side. *But he's begun to grow*, Loxton thought to himself…*he'll need some new clothes*…making a mental note to speak to Pennery about that when they formalised his position as Kip's official guardian now that they had cleared and closed up Miss Harrison's house which would be kept in trust for him.

"Hi Pennery, d'y have a moment to talk about young Kip?"

"Of course."

"Let's get into the office. It's got a big fan." They went inside. Loxton indicated one of the two chairs. "Young Kip, I must say he looks very well."

"Egeria Parroty seems to have a soft spot for both of us," Pennery smiled. "She leaves an evening meal and always something for the weekend. I do breakfast. At midday we do for ourselves, you know bread, fruit, cheese. Most of the children bring something similar, only those who live near enough go home. When the weather gets cold I'll do soup as well."

"Still a bit on the small side, but I think he's grown a little. It occurs to me that he'll need some new clothes, he'll be growing out of those he has."

Pennery nodded, "Been wondering about that. I picked up a catalogue in Parrotys. Seems things can be ordered by post these days. They seem to have everything in there. It has kids' clothes. Even top hats for funerals."

"Well," Loxton paused, "I was talking to Bella, we'll be

going into the city at the beginning of September for a couple of days, 'bout a week before your term begins. She suggests we might take Kip. Get him fitted out. Better than a catalogue. She can make sure it's things big enough for a lad who's growing."

"Good idea, Henry… . What is it, two hundred miles? Kip'll enjoy the train journey, an outing before the new school year begins."

"That's settled. We'll fix dates later." Loxton fidgeted with some papers on his desk. "You happy? Him staying with you?"

"It's fine, no trouble. He's easy to have around. Very self-sufficient for that age. Old Miss Harrison was doing a good job with him."

Loxton looked down at his hands. "Might he be better with a family?"

Pennery thought a moment. "Well I suppose that might be more suitable…Father *and* a mother so to speak…brothers, sisters. Has Kip suggested it? He's not said anything to me but I suppose he might be shy of doing that while he's staying with me…"

"No! No, on the contrary he's very happy with you. You're 'not like a teacher' to quote him." Loxton cleared his throat: "It's just that the Pattersons seem quite keen to adopt him."

"Well, I suppose that could be the best thing for him. Kip might want that, after all his aunt was in the process of adopting him."

"Too true. Final papers for her to sign came through a week after she died and I had to send them back. What about you, Pennery?"

"What *about* me?"

"Had you thought about adopting Kip?"

Pennery froze. "No!" After a long minute, "No. No, as I said, I can't because…no, no I wouldn't want to take on that sort of responsibility…again…for…anyone."

"I just thought that as you are in effect his guardian…which reminds me that ought to be made official as soon as possible."

Pennery stood up. "Look Dill, I'm happy to have him, with me and to look after him, but I'm not intending to *adopt* anyone, now or in the future." He looked hard at Loxton, "Moreover I shall need to think hard whether I want even to become his 'official' guardian come to that. If Kip prefers to live with the Pattersons, then no hard feelings." He gazed out of the window before looking back at Loxton "I was astonished when you said he was coming to me."

"Surely not! After all you must have agreed when he asked you."

"Dill, he never asked me. The first I heard of it was when you told me that he was coming."

"It never occurred to me that he hadn't asked...it was *his* choice."

"If he's changed his mind," Pennery said briskly, "and wants to become the Pattersons' adopted son then he does so with my blessing."

"No, Pennery. He's made no such suggestion. He's never indicated he'd prefer to have the Pattersons as guardians. Between you and me, I think he enjoys living with you. You don't *fuss,* he tells me. I think he suspects, quite correctly I guess, that Patterson would 'fuss' all the time!" Loxton coughed, shuffled some papers and sought hurriedly to move on. "By the way did you know he has a birthday coming up? Must say I thought he was older than that." He pushed a birth certificate across. "But let me know whether you really feel you *can't* be his official guardian. It needs to be settled. I've already suggested to Ottawa that you should be one of the trustees of his aunt's estate. They've agreed on myself, Randall, you and Patterson – 'always good to have a man of the cloth on a Trust' they advised. The old girl left the boy pretty well off and of course there's the house. Egeria Parroty is happy to keep an eye on it, furniture sheeted, etc. Should it be sold? I wonder what Kip would feel."

"Do you think there'll be a prospective buyer? Salter's Creek hardly attracts incomers…if there are any these days."

"No," Loxton agreed. "Not these days. Fifty miles from the nearest town, surrounded by hundreds of miles of forest, the fire risk alone… . Until of course two more prospectors claim to have discovered gold!"

"Nobody would get away with *that* these days," Pennery laughed.

They parted. Loxton stood thoughtful. *Why was Pennery reluctant to become the boy's 'official' guardian? The war?* And as for adoption! Not for the first time he realised how little they knew of the schoolmaster's background. The boy seemed happy enough, a very pleasant and polite kid so why was Pennery so reluctant to take official responsibility? Perhaps the Minister and his wife really were the answer…Bella…could she make discreet inquiries? Loxton had no conception that his initiative would exacerbate Joyce Patterson's worst fears by disinterring the nightmare possibility that the boy would be living with them.

II

JULY

…if it be not now, yet it will come…

7

Summer ripened into a drier and drier series of rainless weeks. Soft brown dykes of vegetation humped like furry caterpillars pushed into position over the heat-hardened ruts of forest tracks by carts hauling lumber. Not a breath disturbed the forest. It was uncannily quiet amongst the trees; a fact remarked on by those whose work took them there. Even Kendall the saw-mill owner, not a particular observant or sensitive man, noticed when he walked some of the long dark lanes which led away from the road. The only movement in the still air, that of dead pine needles sifting down to carpet the dry earth beneath, the only sound, an almost indefinable 'click' as they nicked dry black branches.

It began to grow very hot indeed, building into an unusually desiccating heatwave. Randall noticed Pope Potter seemed to have stopped preaching in the square but paid no more attention apart from observing to his wife that he had missed having the biggest audience of his life by not being at his usual stand when the congregation tumbled out of church some forty minutes early.

The cause, which provided gossip for weeks to come, was not without its amusing side. The organ loft took up the space above the door. In front were two rows of seats, where sat the choir, an autocratic self-elective organisation composed of the twelve nicest-looking children and the twelve most respected ladies in the community. Voice a secondary consideration, they sat in strict order of precedence, children, clean and docile, in front of them, Young Miss Parroty enthroned on a raised bench at the organ behind them all. (The fact that 'Young' Miss Parroty was at least seventy-five did not bother her in the least although nobody had ever dared to refer to her sister Egeria, barely eighteen minutes the elder twin, as Old Miss Parroty.)

She played with questionable skill but commendable agility, manipulating the complexities of the giant organ which were almost as singular as those characterising Pope Potter's harmonium. Most awkward of all were the massive pedals which she could manage only by wearing large flat-heeled shoes. Unkind people had been known to remark that Young Miss Parrotys impressive thighs were a direct result of her organ playing. On every possible occasion she clad herself in an academic robe of eye-dazzling violet which denoted that, many years previously, she had graduated from a long-defunct seat of learning, renowned less for the brilliance of its scholarship than the brilliance of its academic regalia.

The sermon was traditionally the last part of the service, after which came only a very short hymn and The Blessing. It was however preceded by 'The Collection' and, while the plate was passed along each pew, the congregation sang a suitably doleful hymn which however slow, rarely lasted long enough, thus making it necessary for Young Miss Parroty to 'improvise'. On this occasion she had just finished the last verse of a paralysingly drawn-out *Praise My Soul the King of Heaven*, her version of which was distinguished by a much-prolonged pause between the syllables of *Heav...en* and she had embarked enthusiastically on the thunderous improvisation which she had been *"perfecting for three weeks"* as she explained later.

Loxton, in his capacity as Senior Church Warden, had just

begun descending the wooden stairs from the organ-loft, with brimming collection plate, when there came a brief but alarming rending sound. Young Miss Parroty faltered, struck a fistful of wrong notes, before recovering herself again without more than a bad waver. The rending came again even louder, far more prolonged, crescendoing into a roar accompanied by muffled shrieks and a most appalling clattering crash, while choking, clouds of dust obliterated the light. After a few moments of stunned immobility the choir, adults and children crowded round to gaze down at the debris. In her haste Young Miss Parroty snagged her gaily coloured academicals somewhere on the organ which emitted a mournful wail as if in sympathy.

The staircase leading from the gallery had collapsed beneath Loxton's comfortable bulk although, to do him justice, the stairs themselves were old and dry, the wooden pegs that had held them into the wall having shrunk loose. Children managed to scramble down, but the ladies and organist had to be rescued by the fire-fighters' mobile ladder. Patterson abandoned his sermon as he galloped over to take charge of rescue operations gabbling The Blessing to end the service as he did so, although it is doubtful anyone was listening.

As if some mortally wounded prehistoric monster in its death throes, the organ continued to howl, a noise so deafening that they had to shout to make themselves heard until somebody thought to take out a fuse. Cessation of the noise took everyone by surprise not least Kip. Catching at Pennery's arm, he pointed at the choral ladies clinging fearfully to the front rail of their balcony stage-whispering the refrain of a currently popular ditty: in the sudden silence *'There we sits like bird in the wilderness'* rang out like a treble solo. It broke the tension raising smiles and chuckles from the less devout thankful to be released early, without having to suffer another interminable sermon.

Patterson however was not amused; it provided further proof of Pennery's over-indulgent guardianship.

Although Loxton was not too badly damaged, he was immobilised for two days with bruises and a badly twisted ankle. Maguire sent his recently employed part-time reporter to interview anyone (which was almost everyone) who had anything to say, although several subversive observations to the effect that it was probably Young Miss Parrotys over-enthusiastic improvisation which proved the last straw for the organ loft were never published.

Not very long after what *The Sentinel* headlined as **ORGAN LOFT CALAMITY** (the only way it could manage to fit in an emboldened large-font banner) Kip Harrison was dawdling past the 'Mayor's' office. It was excruciatingly hot, and at three o'clock in the afternoon there was nobody else about.

"Hey Kip, y'got a moment?"

"Somethin' I'c'n do, Mr Loxton?" Kip poked his head through open doorway.

"I was wondering if you'd drop this note along at The Manse." He was licking envelope in great slow licks. "Nobody else here on a Saturday and I've still got this." He pointed to his foot and bandaged leg.

It occurred to Kip that Loxton might have telephoned but, having nothing else to do, he was glad of the job. He had never seen inside the Pattersons' house and possessed an intelligent ten-year-old's curiosity, furthermore on such a hot day was there not the chance of cool lemonade?

Loxton was ruffled, not only by the embarrassing fact that he had vanished from sight so ludicrously in a cloud of beetle-chewed-wood dust, but because for over a year Patterson had been warning him that the collapse of the stairs was imminent.

Even as he was languishing in bed, there had come a missive from Patterson suggesting that Loxton **might now see his way to persuading Salter's Creek that urgent repair of the organ loft was a community responsibility.** Its bluntly sarcastic tone, adding insult to injury, inclined him to refuse outright and although he knew full well that he could not fob off Patterson for ever, he could at least show his irritation by taking his own good time to put the proposition on the agenda of the relevant committee. He had not forgotten the telephone but, for the time being, he was deliberately avoiding personal contact with Patterson – hence entrusting his prevaricating reply to Kip.

Kip pulled on the bell of the big house near the church. It did not work. He knocked, but it made little sound and he hurt his knuckle on the hard-baked wood. He was about to put the letter on the sill of a window beside the door when he felt the door move against his shoulder. It swung open. Curiosity was too much for him; he stepped in. There was nowhere except the floor to leave the letter.

A sense of adventure transformed the whole errand into the hazardous undercover expedition of a daring Special Messenger delivering Top Secret information to the Master Spy and Double Agent known only as 'P'. Through the crack of a door ajar on the right he could see a window and a big shiny dark-wood table. He pushed it open softly. Patterson's study was a wide neat room with books in cases all-round the walls. The table was empty. He put the letter in the middle where it stood out, a white rectangle on the black surface. A snuffling noise made him start. Asleep in the sun in a chair behind a desk by the window was Patterson, hair oddly ruffled against the high back. Taking a moment from making notes, he had pushed his spectacles up on his forehead and dozed off in the heat of the afternoon.

Should he wake him? No! Surely 'P' would expect the note to have arrived by An Unseen Hand. Kip tiptoed quietly away, sliding quietly out of the room, then with exaggerated caution across the hall. He edged round the front door in case there was an enemy agent outside waiting to follow him. Coast clear, pulling an imaginary hat low over his brow, he stepped quickly through the porch and slunk low against the hedge to the front gate. Mission Accomplished. Back now in the guise of a boy the Special Messenger ran smoothly down the dusty road before digging his hands deep into his pockets and slowing to a walk.

Loxton's question came back to him. Yes, he supposed not everyone would want to lodge with his schoolmaster, but he couldn't think of Pennery like that. He'd never had any siblings but most of the other boys had and, from what he could make out, Pennery treated him more like a younger brother. He was by nature an easy child, refreshingly able to look after himself, tidy and personally responsible by nature. His aunt had complimented him on the fact that she never had to tell him to wash his hands, clean his teeth, or that it was about time he had a bath.

Joyce Patterson had returned a little earlier than usual from her regular Saturday shopping trip. She felt the heat rather badly and, taking her way back home across a piece of waste land overgrown by a mass of sweet-smelling weed, the heady scent made her almost drowsy. Heavily laden with two baskets she arrived at last at the back of the house. The kitchen door stood open, the house waited blessedly dark and cool. A slight current of air fanned her, she could see the front door too was partially open. Thankfully she rested both baskets on the kitchen table. She must soon set about preparing for guests that evening... though because of her fear for his reputation she was astonished her husband had invited the Randalls...and was about to seat herself for a moment when, his back towards her, Kip Harrison, emerged from her husband's study. She did not move. Could not move. Now cold as ice she watched him stepped quietly … *surreptitiously…*through the hall. *He doesn't wish to be seen!* By the time he reached the front door she had half-convinced herself that rather than fear or even revulsion at whatever had taken place, his stealthy exit denoted guilt…almost as if… *Should she call out and settle it once and for all?* but in that instant he'd slipped round the door and was gone. On the spur of the moment she hurried, along the hall after him and out onto the garden path… *perhaps an offer of lemonade might allow her to make a more accurate assessment of the state of affairs…*but when she reached the gate she saw he was already running away.

She did not call after him. She shut the door and heard her husband move in the study. The wild hope that the boy might have sneaked in to steal something in her husband's temporary absence faded. Leonard was there in the study and though stealthy the boy had not seemed upset…almost as if… . *Could it be the boy was complicit?*

Joyce Patterson went softly back to the kitchen and dissolved into a fit of deep, quiet weeping. Everything had begun to go so well after the fuss over the wretched boy's absence from church her husband had not so much as mentioned him again and his silence on the matter had begun to reassure her. *Should she not have interpreted his sudden lack of comment as sinister?* Now, at a stroke, fear and disgust was once again uppermost. Her weekly shopping trip was a regular affair. Today, because of the heat she had cut it short and thus arrived home earlier than usual…what she had witnessed was evidently a pre-planned assignation… . Had Leonard and the boy been seeing each other…? Regularly…? Every Saturday?

It was almost four, she steadied herself, made tea and put the chipped brown pot with cups and milk on a tray and she felt calmer. Was there not after all, another, more rational entirely innocent explanation? Perhaps the boy had come with a message? But if so, why sneak out and run away?

"How's the sermon, dear?" She placed the tray on the mahogany table in the study where they always had tea on a Saturday. She knew her face was blotchy and hoped he would not notice or, if he did, would put it down to the heat. She busied herself pouring the tea.

"How's it going, dear?"

Although her voice had a forced brightness it escaped Patterson, deep as he now was in the sermon over which he had fallen asleep. "Going very well. Yes, very well I think." Then, as the thought struck him for the first time, "I suppose I could have used the one that I was prevented from using last week on account of the 'Calamity'! However, it is always as well to have something new to say and for me to keep up my Saturday sermon-writing habit."

"And how is little Kip getting on?" She chirruped it like a sparrow on a hedge, each word lodging with peculiar precision in the hot still air, her fingers clattering the tea-cups which irritated her husband who loathed sharp sounds of any sort.

"Kip? Oh, *Kip* – Young Harrison? Yes. Well enough." He paused. "Oh yes, well enough I imagine… . As far as I know, even though that Pennery…but of course I haven't actually spoken to the boy." He was puzzled at the inconsequentiality of her enquiry, by her apparent change of subject. Usually at Saturday tea-time he explained his sermon to her and she made suggestions for improving it – nothing radical, possibly a word or two changed. Patterson liked to think that he could take adverse criticism. "As you know, the boy's welfare is *not* allowed to be *any* concern of ours. None at all. Unfortunately. I made my offer, but that Pennery obviously felt that as the boy's schoolmaster…enough said!"

"Your sermon, dear, is it finished ? I mean, did it take you all afternoon?"

"Yes Joyce it's finished…well almost." *Her voice had a curious tone.* "I worked hard at it all morning. In this heat even thinking's a strain and it took every moment I had."

"When I came in I thought…" She almost faced him with it, but courage failed her at the last moment.

He remembered he had dozed off. Of course! She had come in with Loxton's letter and found him asleep glasses pushed up on his forehead. *It must have been her shutting of the front door or her movements back in the kitchen that roused me.* The thought of being caught out in an untruth however slight flustered him. Quite unaware that she had entirely misinterpreted his momentary embarrassment, he said hurriedly, "Perhaps you think I didn't hear you come in? I wasn't *really* asleep it was…"

"Of course not, dear." Her voice brittle, flat.

"It was simply that…"

For an instant she wondered if he was going to confide in her.

"That…well let's say I may have had *twenty* winks?" But the rest of the time I really was sermonising." She offered no response.

"Do you know, Joyce, Loxton says he *won't* raise a Rate to repair the organ loft? He does go on so! Suggests the congregation must raise a special fund to pay for the repair!" Then, attempting to lighten the atmosphere by waving the offending missive and reading aloud in a deliberately boring voice the letter he supposed his wife had delivered whilst he was having his nap, "I ask you isn't *that* enough to send *anyone* to sleep?"

She on her part, having no idea that there had been any letter delivered, assumed that he was trying to change the topic of conversation. It imbued her with a moment's determination.

"*I* saw Kip today, Leonard. I *saw* Kip Harrison *today*."

He looked at her in astonishment. Had she not herself, only minutes ago, asked him if *he* had seen Kip and whether he thought the boy was well?

"You didn't realise I'd seen him, did you?"

"Ah…no, dear…I had no idea you'd seen him." *What if she had?*

"Leonard, did you leave the door on the latch? The front door I mean?"

Another abrupt change of subject! Perhaps heat was affecting her, after all she had walked back, laden with shopping as usual he supposed. "I suppose I may have done. I really don't know."

"It was open last week too. *Last Saturday?* Left on the latch? I shut it today." She really was looking at him very strangely. *Was she afraid they might be robbed? Here? In Salter's Creek!* "And don't forget Leonard that I saw the boy *today.*" There was a brief silence as she gathered the tea-tray and went out.

Open last week? He had no idea whether it had been left on the latch. Kip Harrison? *Was she implying that the boy's a sneak thief?* In all their married life he had never heard her so enigmatic.

After a time he abandoned trying to sort it out there and then. Finishing his sermon was the immediate problem. He glanced again at Loxton's letter. This Sunday he would conclude by emphasising the expense of the repair was an urgent *community* responsibility, making a point of asking Loxton to take the Collection directly *after* his sermon on this occasion, thus putting him at a moral disadvantage. After all, how could Loxton walk round collecting offerings and not be prepared to do his bit by raising an emergency Rate to repair the organ-loft?

Patterson fetched his pipe and filled it from the tobacco jar. He allowed himself one smoke a week, after he had finished the sermon. A wave of good fellowship washed over him as he drew in a mouthful of the scented smoke. The heat of the day lessened into a pleasant early-evening warmth. He would open a bottle of wine. A luxury he enjoyed although he would never have admitted it. Perhaps two bottles on such a hot evening?

Earlier in the month he had invited the policeman and his wife to supper, only to discover that for some unexplained reason his wife seemed reluctant to entertain the Randalls and was equally unenthusiastic about accepting invitations from them. As he mused he was forced to admit she no longer seemed her once-equable self; there could be no doubt that she was in a state of tension. She had been particularly nervy for several weeks which he had put down to the unusually high temperatures coming on top of the longest dry spell Salter's Creek had experienced for several years. Now she seemed have a bee in her bonnet about young Harrison. Did she feel sorry for him losing his great aunt so soon after his parents? Perhaps he should not have made so much fuss over the boy's Sunday truancy? However on reflection he realised it was far longer-standing. When had begun? He cast his mind back to old Miss Harrison's death and their offer to undertake the boy's guardianship. Could it really be that?

He snatched his pipe halfway from his mouth. *Of course!* No wonder his wife seemed so on edge, harping-on about seeing the boy as she had that very afternoon. *It was entirely his fault.* He had pushed to the back of his mind the fact he had led her to hope that they would be able to adopt the boy, thus giving her at last the child she so longed for. More than that, he had perhaps let her take for granted that by now he would have already been in their care and his own current doubts as to Pennery's suitability as guardian had re-awakened her longing.

How could he have been so insensitive?! She had always wanted a child. As the Minister's wife she must have believed there would be no difficulty at all in adopting Kip. If, 'Mayor' Loxton had decided, as it seemed he had, that the boy should continue to stay with the schoolmaster, then he Leonard Patterson, the

Minister, would also make a decision: the Harrison boy was not the only orphan in the world needing foster parents.

The dinner party (though any meal after four in the afternoon was usually called 'supper', *lunch'* being unknown in Salter's Creek) found Patterson in a buoyant mood and even Randall was sounding more cheerful: no fires of any sort had been reported despite the rainless month and there were forecasts of thunderstorms which would greatly lessen any fire-risk. The evening was warm without being uncomfortable; the room illuminated by candles in two simple but impressive three-branched candlesticks inherited from Joyce's mother encouraged a relaxed atmosphere.

Randall chivvied Patterson good-naturedly about the wine which gleamed deep red in their glasses, suggesting that he was sybaritic, comparing 'poor policemen' to 'well-wined prelates'. Though at other times he might have been more on his dignity Patterson was in the mood to take it all in good part. He was bubbling over, buoyed by the knowledge that Joyce, who seemed unusually reserved at the table, would be thrilled by his decision, certain the surprise itself would revive her spirits instantly and dispel her moodiness.

Just before the end of the meal, he cleared his throat loudly and tapped his glass. They looked at him rather surprised.

"What's this? Speeches?" Randall asked.

"A speech, no," Patterson was enjoying himself, "but an announcement, yes!"

Something alerted Joyce Patterson and she tried to frown warningly at him, but he seemed, or perhaps chose, not to notice. *Had he had been drinking rather more than was judicious?*

"As you probably know," his face clouded for an instant, "we offered to have young Harrison when his aunt died." He caught his wife's eye, appalled to see all colour drain from her face and so as not to let her dwell on her disappointment continued quickly, "What you may not know is that we had really been looking forward to the idea of giving the boy a home, having him here with us in our house as part of a family." His wife looked livid in the candle-light, her lips black gashes. He hurried on so as not to prolong her agony. "In view of the fact that Pennery may not perhaps be proving to be the ideal guardian I had suggested to Henry Loxton that maybe he should think again and that the Harrison boy would after all be better off in a home with a father and *mother* as it were." Joyce gave a little gasp. "However as I gather that may not happen, I have decided that we shall take steps to adopt a boy. The church has a society and…" With a smashing of glass and a dimming of light as one of the candlesticks toppled, Joyce Patterson collapsed across the table.

8

i

The promised thunderstorms did not materialise. Joyce Patterson, fainting so dramatically at her dinner party, seemed to be only the first of several victims of the heatwave, mainly women and younger children, those who normally spent a large part of their time indoors and could be badly affected by even an afternoon in the sun. These casualties started a fashion in large straw hats which were called 'donkey-hats' because somebody had received a postcard from a distant relation in Italy which showed a horse wearing a sun hat. Parrotys had to get in new stocks and, before everyone was supplied, it was nothing to see otherwise staid matrons with their heads protected by large white handkerchiefs protecting their necks.

Children especially took to it all in a big way. One very small girl found at home a yellowing *solar-topée* dating from the previous century so large that she looked like a walking toadstool and was reluctant to take it off even at school. From another abandoned drawer in his room, Kip Harrison unearthed a battered straw-boater with faded Oxford college ribbon belonging to Pennery who told him he looked like the rakish juvenile lead in a Broadway musical, though Kip had only the haziest idea of what a 'Broadway' musical was.

Summer continued to burn its way relentlessly into every facet of life, hats were not the only outward manifestation of the community's response to intolerable heat. So few people shopped in the daytime that Parrotys Store closed at midday, opening instead at five o'clock for four hours in the evening and, because by mid-morning it was stiflingly hot inside the church, Patterson took to holding the Sunday service in the evening rather than morning. Pope Potter appeared to have deserted McCutcheon Square entirely on Sundays although he was glimpsed occasionally on a forest track, or furiously pedalling his bizarre harmonium-altar through the town very early in the morning on weekdays, the great black dog loping behind him.

As well as domestic quarters, the school consisted of Big Schoolroom in which Pennery taught. Fewer girls than boys attended and were instructed mornings only by Bella Loxton in Small Schoolroom. On the whole they were the younger ones; their older sisters were 'home educated'– learning to cook, look after babies and toddlers, undertake domestic chores as would befit future wives and mothers.

Nobody from Salter's Creek went away for holidays in the summer, nor at any other time for that matter. By far the greater part of the population consisted of families in outlying settlements who made their living from the ground their forebears had hacked from virgin forest, seasonally supplemented by logging and trapping, and it was inconvenient to have children at home for too long, thus Pennery's inspired suggestion that the summer term and vacation should be integrated had been warmly welcomed. He had proposed beginning the Summer Term mid-April, continuing to mid-May with a First Vacation Break lasting until the end of the month, then the school re-opening on the first of June until mid-July and the Second Vacation Break until the end of July. The school would re-open for the whole of August followed by the Third Vacation Break for the first fortnight in September with the new school year beginning in the middle of that month as usual.

Not yet the end of July, still no rain, none expected, tension increased: normally mild-tempered men swore at each other in the course of the daily round. Although the lofty schoolrooms were airy and relatively cool even at midday children too began to show signs of strain resulting in occasional bad-tempered scuffles. Fortunately there were only days to go before Pennery's novel vacation arrangement began.

There came rumours of a forest fire further west. Everyone took to glancing surreptitiously at the rim of the forest in the evenings, dreading they would see the tell-tale glow of a major conflagration. Randall was manifestly uneasy. The fact that there had not even been the usual minor conflagrations, occasioned by some careless motorist brewing up or a stray shaft of sun magnified by a shard of glass from a shattered bottle, seemed somehow ominous rather than reassuring, as if Fate was hinting that it had something far worse in store.

Although that was not Maguire's intention, *The Sentinel's* editorials heightened the general unease by putting into words what Salter's Creek instinctively preferred to ignore. It had been *The Sentinel* which had originally proposed the observation platform at Three Pines Rough should be fitted with an amplifying system so that, in case of a fire everyone could be kept abreast of the situation. Now it recommended that each small-holding should ensure it had a fire-proof shelter partly dug into the ground and covered by a good thick layer of earth, turf, stones in which to store containers and buckets filled with fresh drinking water. However helpful they were meant to be, these editorial suggestions, sensible though they were, served to increase rather than lessen anxieties.

It was therefore unfortunate that the suggestion that **erection of an asbestos roof would protect fire-watchers on the platform at Three Pines Rough from falling cinders** should provoke Loxton to remark dismissively, "Not much use having a fire*proof* roof supported by three extremely fire-*prone* trees!' A subsequent rather pained admonitory editorial, whilst admitting that on its rocky outcrop Salter's Creek as a tree-free oasis **was certainly too sparsely vegetated to be anything but a natural firebreak,** further increased anxiety when it went on to point out some houses, **especially those long boarded-up round McCutcheon Square will be in imminent danger from drifting sparks.** It concluded unhelpfully **by far the greatest hazard to life will be the raw, scorching, cinder-strewn air in our lungs.** Fears hitherto secretly harboured became far more menacing and imminent once voiced in print.

ii

His glimpse of the birth certificate had reminded Pennery that Kip was coming up for his eleventh birthday. Loxton was not alone in assuming he must have been older; the loss, first of his parents and aunt, had aged him beyond his years. There should be a party, Pennery decided and arranged for the elder Miss Parroty (an acknowledged festive-cake maker) to bake a large cake.

It was a time of the year strangely barren of birthdays amongst the children and, very conveniently, Kip's fell on the Friday which began the second of the innovative fortnightly summer vacation breaks with a half-day. It took on the nature of a general celebration, promising momentary relief from the growing fear of the forest fire further west. Thus it developed from a party for children into an informal party for their parents too, although there was a tacit understanding that nothing stronger than a local cider was to be provided for the adults.

Those who lived too far away to go home for their midday meal helped Pennery make over Big Schoolroom as the venue for a film which he had hired for an aged projector which had been acquired, nobody knew how, by his long-vanished predecessor. Illumination, provided by an alarmingly hot acetylene flame melted the celluloid if the film jammed as it often did, moreover it gave off considerable heat adding to the already stifling atmosphere.

Appropriately enough, considering the origins of Salter's Creek, it was an early version of *The Gold Rush* and a silent version at that. Although *The Jazz Singer* had appeared a couple of years earlier the Randalls and the Loxtons were the only local people familiar with 'talkies'. However, entering into the spirit of the occasion, Loxton undertook to provide a piano accompaniment; he had been a popular silent-film pianist in his younger days and his extemporised, if slightly faltering, tunes seemed admirably suited to the occasion.

Leonard Patterson, as one of Kip's trustees, joined in the celebration with the rest and everyone waited for him to finish a rather longer Grace than the occasion called for. Joyce was still confined to bed, quite unwell according to Dr Svensson who had to drive fifty miles to see her. He was a comparative stranger in Salter's Creek which had previously relied on Kip's aunt for medical advice. Had anyone thought to ask, he could have told them that although she had read medicine, passing every exam with distinction, as a woman she had been unable to qualify as a doctor but had indeed served both in Mesopotamia and on the Western Front, a highly respected Queen Alexandra's Army Nursing Service Matron whose medical understanding was greatly superior to young newly qualified army doctors who frequently sought her advice.

Almost dusk when Patterson finished Grace, they moved to Small Schoolroom where an impressive display of food awaited them on wooden trestle tables draped (at Egeria Parrotys insistence) with freshly laundered sheets pulled down to the floor and tucked under the table-legs.

Kip shyly showed off his birthday presents to an admiring audience, particularly proud of the horn-handled sheath-knife the Miss Parrotys had given him that morning. These knives, with wickedly sharp blades, although available from Parrotys Store and widely used by adults were not regarded as toys. None of his contemporaries had one; Kip saw it as recognition that he was no longer regarded as a little boy.

At the far end of the room, below the big window, dominating a mouth-watering array of tarts, cream cakes, buns, biscuits and a wonderful selection of sandwiches, stood a magnificent cake at the centre of a white-swathed table so wide that, without standing on a chair, Kip was unable to reach far enough across to blow out the eleven candles – which he did in one breath to affectionate applause.

The momentary expectant hush which precedes a real spree, was broken by a small girl at the back being *shhusshed*, but her whimper became more insistent and somehow prolonged the silence.

"But Mammy, I don't *like* ants."

First the rear rows, then the front turned towards the still open door at the back. The white-painted step was infested with ants; they spread from side to side of the threshold, crawling quickly down into the room.

"Mammy, I can *hear* them!"

Like the stirring of dry leaves, or sweep of a bridal dress up the aisle, came the unnerving rustle of thousands of minute feet across the centre of the room. A sigh shuddered through the watchers and a preparatory movement.

"STAND STILL!" Sensing imminent panic, Pennery transfixed them with his shout. "Listen," he insisted. "Listen to me and do as I say. Keep back against the walls. Keep right back. Don't disturb them. Don't divert them. They're on the march and they'll go straight through. Kip," he turned to where, like the others, the boy stood fascinated by the advancing black column. "Kip, open that window above the table and then stand back against the wall." The situation was so nightmarish that there was no murmur of protest, even from the adults. Pennery continued without raising his voice. "Hold onto smaller children. We're quite all right if we let them go through. When a colony is on the move, they're always very well disciplined."

A black undulating column poured into the room, a wide sinuous ebony ribbon reaching ever forward from the doorway. Pennery was right, the column never became any wider; along either flank warder-ants ran to and fro pushing back into line those who strayed. It seemed as if nobody was breathing, the only sound the whisper of tiny feet over clean dry floorboards. Then, as though at a word of command the whispering feet stopped as one, halted by the white wall barring their way.

Two or three ants, acting as scouts or guides, went cautiously forward, curious, wary. First one, then another climbed the sheet-swathed table legs in a tentative exploratory manner until they reached the top. The utter silence broken by a small boy crying out excitedly, "Look, they've come to the party!" which would have been funny had the spectacle not been so horrifically hypnotic.

As if at a further command, the entire column moved forward again, following the advance-guard. The black tide rose up the sheeted table in its path and swept over it, over plates, over cakes, birthday-candle-light gleaming on black legs and bodies.

On went the pathfinders through the window which Kip had opened. Still the outriders controlled the column, maintaining compact disciplined ranks across the food which lay in their path.

"They're eating it *all!*" came a childish voice, aghast at seeing his tea vanish before his eyes.

One of the smoking candles lurched and fell. Pennery said evenly, "Keep calm. They'll only eat what's there in their path."

The black cohort began to sink lower as, fragment by fragment, the food they passed over was devoured. Pennery looked back to the door, still they flowed in. Two or three very young children began to weep softly, "Let them cry," Pennery murmured, "but hang onto 'em."

Candles toppled. Some ants were incinerated but it did not interrupt the onward progress for they were borne off by their comrades out into the night. A broad rippling ribbon stretching from door to window. There must have been millions of them.

At last, after almost twenty minutes, the doorway was clear. As if rolling up a blind, the rear-guard ushered the last of the dark horde up the hall, over the tables through the window until they vanished, every single one of them, into the waiting night. An owl whooped once as if bidding them farewell.

Nobody spoke.

One plate lay wiped clean except for a single fallen still-smoking candle but most unnerving of all was the precisely controlled width of the damage to the remaining food, extending only as far as the edges of the column, not a crumb further. Well over half the great cake had been devoured as completely and cleanly as if sliced by a new-honed knife leaving only a few half-nibbled sugar petals amidst the debris of metal, wax and wire of fallen decorative birthday-candle holders. Halved cakes and half tarts lay eerily untouched; the side of one jam sponge had vanished leaving the rest like an eclipsed planet. Not a single ant remained in sight.

The guests left.

Without a word they disappeared into the night as noiselessly as the ants. Pennery did not even suggest that they should tackle the untouched food.

It remained stifling, hot and still outside and uncannily silent. Kip and Pennery watched them go before turning back to the schoolhouse without exchanging a word. Momentarily Kip caught at Pennery's hand and Pennery gave it a reassuring squeeze. For that instant a fragile bridge was built but, as if each for his own private reason was unwilling to accept the responsibilities which ties of affection might demand, it was only a fleeting moment of intimacy.

The following day Salter's Creek experienced an equally sudden invasion of snakes – snakes of every shape, marking and size. They appeared in houses and gardens, several were killed. Some people saw three or four dozen in the space of half an hour. Maguire found two in the printing office. Loxton was besieged with telephone calls. They vanished almost as mysteriously as they had arrived.

Pennery thought that they, like the ants, appeared to be moving eastward, but he said nothing to anyone except Randall. That evening, neither of them was surprised that the previous rumours of a big fire about a hundred and ten miles west of Salter's Creek were confirmed. The following day fire-watchers on the platform at Three Pines Rough could see smoke like great thunder clouds hovering on the far distant horizon; fortunately there was no breath of wind to drive it in their direction.

The heatwave continued. Day after day sun scorched down. Wooden buildings cracked open. Paint split. Dust lay nearly a foot deep in the gutters. By midday tin pipes and roofing were hot enough to fry eggs; cool evenings seemed a myth of a past age. Only deep in the forest was there any real relief from the implacable sun and even there it was hot and dry as the open door of an oven, with fallen twigs and branches snapping underfoot, crackling like flames on a hearth.

Joyce Patterson improved but seemed never fully to recover. She became very silent. Her husband noticed how tense she seemed, how her eyes followed him everywhere, how she started at each knock at the door. School restarted. Twice Kip brought a message from Pennery suggesting, in view of the heat, amendments to the timing of religious education classes, even suggesting cancellation; each time she went into hysterics. Patterson assumed the boy's appearance reminded her of his promise. He had taken the first step by writing to the adoption society he had mentioned at the dinner-party and was prepared to wait. He would make no further reference to it until there was something definite, something positive to tell her. Quite apart from anything else, they could not undertake an adoption with her in such an overwrought state. He was relieved to see she was beginning to creep about again though nervously, but noticed she now rarely left the house, even on Saturday… *especially on Saturday?*

One morning he realised with a shock that not only were there very distinct streaks of grey in her dark formerly lustrous hair, but she had become far less meticulous about her personal appearance. Svensson visited again. Although a conscientious doctor, he was based too far away to observe her as often as he might have wished but finally, albeit somewhat reluctantly, he agreed with Patterson that it was most probably her wish for children that lay at the root of the problem. Neither he nor her husband were aware that, little by little, day by day, Joyce Pennery was losing her reason.

9

Splash-Puddle lay deep in the forest about four miles from the town centre. It was in fact the only bathing place and used only by boys; no girl had ever been known to take a dip there. Fathers took their sons at about the age of eight, older brothers introduced their younger siblings. It was perhaps the nearest thing to a 'coming of age' tradition that Salter's Creek could boast.

Kip walked there after school one afternoon, thinking about the ants and the snakes. He was astonished, but pleased, to discover it deserted, he had expected some of the other boys to be there already. The surrounding trees stood back, as if respectfully, on each side; white sand at the bottom looked invitingly cool, the fringing bushes fresh and green in contrast to the brown-tinged undergrowth elsewhere. There was not the slightest breeze. The forest was uncannily quiet, as if holding its breath in expectation of some unguessed-at happening, the only sound a bubbling hiss as the spring squeezed through its narrow fissure, preventing utter silence.

It seemed wrong to disturb the peace with hurry and bustle. He began to undress very slowly, first his snake-buckle belt with the precious sheath-knife, then shirt, shorts, sneakers, depositing them neatly as a military kit-layout beneath a very tall deciduous tree of indeterminate family before stepping carefully over bristly short grass towards the water. The pool, never quite still because of the flow in and out, wavered like a huge distorting mirror revealing him stark-naked except for the musical-comedy headgear. Laughing at himself, he took it off and tossed it beside the clothes then, thinking better of it, trotted back, took the knife from its sheath, drove it into the tree as a makeshift hat-peg. However, over-hastily turning back to the pool, he failed to notice the boater sliding off onto the carefully piled clothes.

For almost five minutes he stood watching his reflection; the slow-moving water accentuated the corrugations of his ribs as he breathed in and out, flexing first his belly, then his thighs. His body was not bad as bodies went, he supposed; not skinny but not fat; tanned arms and legs highlighted against the whiteness of the rest of his body made the contrast greater.

It was the sort of evening when the air itself is almost sensuous. He looked down at himself. Nothing. Last year he had noticed older boys had hair down there. One of them seeing him staring had laughed, "It'll happen to you too…when you can…" repeatedly moving his half-clenched fist. Kip held himself similarly, tentatively imitating the mystifying movement. He repeated the gesture more quickly, felt himself sticking up, stiffening to a erect tenderness which urged him to prolong a seductively exquisite sensation he had never ever previously experienced which momentarily excited but also alarmed him so much that he hastily released himself. *Was this what the laughing boy meant?* Looking down at himself again he found himself in some strange way unsure whether he should feel disappointed or relieved that there was still no sign of any hair.

He stretched his hands out in front of him: livid scars, legacy of the accident in which his parents had died. At the edge of the pool, water lapping his feet, he crouched down and fingered his toes. Even in the cool water he could almost feel again that moment of fierce pain. In the garden aged four, barefooted as he was now, he had rushed forward 'to help' just as his father drove down the garden fork to break up a hard clayey sod, one sharp prong skewering each small foot.

He straightened and walked into the water, very slowly so as not to disturb his reflections more than necessary. A shiver of pleasure. The water, though very slightly warmed by the sun during the day, seemed enticingly cool as it licked hot dusty flesh at each step. He stopped several times just to allow himself to feel the exquisite difference between that part of him above and that below the water. The cool touch took his knee, another step, his thigh, groin, belly, ribs. He stood there at the deepest point and, deciding to recapture it walked quickly through to the shallows on the far side and then, just as slowly as before, back to the centre.

However the pleasurable sensations of that initial immersion were absent and now he even felt slightly cold as he stood back on the bank. He decided to run in and swim the few strokes possible before having to stand up when it got too shallow. That was when he realised that somebody had been watching.

How long Pope Potter had been there was difficult to say. He was so still that he might well have seen the whole proceedings; without the familiar bent top-hat he no longer seemed the comic caricature of an eccentric preacher but the epitome of an authoritative Old Testament prophet. He regarded the boy with the intensity an older child might have found embarrassing but Kip, still too young and unaware to be self-conscious of his nakedness, merely waved,

"Hi!"

The old man came forward into the edge of pool, beckoning until they were standing face to face in the shallows. Suddenly he was right up close. Kip wrinkled his nose, the hem of old man's grubby robe, now awash, gave off an unfamiliar, sour, body smell. Taken by surprise, Kip tried to step away only to find his shoulders held, firmly but with such infinite gentleness the flash of fear departed. According to some of the other boys, Pope Potter was said to have a hoard of gold dust which, over the years, he'd panned from some secret claim deep in the forests. Perhaps the old man was going to let him into the secret, tell him where to find it?

"Yes! Yes! Yes, *Thy* Father which Art in Heaven." The old man removed his hands from the boy's shoulders, gently touching hair, cheeks and lip before, almost reverently, taking them down the boy's arms. Then, taking hold of Kip's hands he scrutinised each one for a long moment, first the back, then the palm, fingering the scars, nodding several times as if it confirmed something he already knew.

Blunt, thick, dirty, wrinkled fingers, but smooth as silk, lighter than feathers stroked ribs, waist, flanks, thighs, calves as if the old man needed to assure to assure himself the boy really existed in the flesh. Finally, kneeling, he stared intently down through the bright still clear water which only just covered the boy's feet. The lividity of the scar in the middle of each foot contrasted shockingly with the untanned surrounding flesh.

"I was four...had to have stitches." *Why did he feel the need to explain? Was the old man even listening?*

Nodding to himself, Pope Potter straightened, sitting back on his heels, gazing out across the water, eyes oddly glazed as though waking from a long, drugged sleep.

"The Time is Come *Now!*" Still clad in his robe, he stood, took the boy gently by the wrist and, as if it were part of some predetermined ceremony, led Kip deeper into the pool, the cool water gradually reaching up as if it were a supernatural presence stroking the top of his thighs.

Kip was neither frightened nor amused. If anything he was sobered by the circumstances and setting: windless peace of surrounding trees, vividness of vegetation which seemed to have absorbed extra greenness from early evening light, crystal-clear water lipping the edge of the pool before vanishing into nether regions as effortlessly as it had it had emerged.

A solitary shaft of late sunlight lay like a silk scarf flung across bushes, abandoned clothes and gleaming water, flaming Pope Potter's face, beard, hair. There amongst the tall pines as light began to fail, Kip was awed by the situation in which he found himself; the unreality moved him in way he did not understand, could not comprehend. *Another part of growing older, like growing hair down there?*

If he was unaware of the absurdity, the pathos of the scene, he was unaware too of its disturbing intensity: a small boy quite naked, evening sun transforming droplets of water in his hair as if they were sparkling diamonds enhancing a golden crown and an old man enveloped in a soggy dirty-white robe, grey head now a silver aureole in the fading light, facing each other in a forest pool as a long hot afternoon faded into evening.

Pope Potter took his baked-bean-tin chalice from the breast of his robe and dipped it in the water. Lifting it high above his head with both hands he then dribbled it over of the boy's head. Once. Twice. Three times.

"You Are My Beloved Son, In Whom I Am Well Pleased."

Were the words were being addressed to him? Kip did not hear them distinctly enough to be sure. He was beginning to feel chilled. Did Pope Potter think he, Kip, was his *son*? That must be it! The old man had a long-lost son and imagined...

"Com'st *Thou* to *Me*?" The old man sounded almost elated then, his mind sliding far away, he sighed, "*I* have great need to be Baptized of *Thee*."

"It *is* me he's talking to,' Kip muttered aloud. *Some sort of game? And now it was his turn to pour water over Pope Potter?* "But I don't know how..."

The old man looked at him eyes ablaze, "Bless *me*! Bless me *Now!*"

Intimidated, Kip lifted a hand in imitation of the old man, said in panic, "Bless-you-bless-you-bless-you." Then, dimly remembering the funerals of his great aunt and his parents, "Dust to dust...Ashes to..." He paused, before gabbling, "In-th'name-of-the-Father-an'ov-the-Son..." finally, with relief... "Amen!" It was the best he could manage.

By now he felt thoroughly chilled; the whole pointless game seemed to have gone on far too long. Out of the water, shivering on the bank, it was darker than he'd realised. He realised too that, having intended to dry in the last of the sun, he had no towel. He wiped off the worst of the water with his shirt, pulling on his clothes so hurriedly that they clung awkwardly to his still-damp body; his shirt pulled under his arms, the shorts chafed his crutch.

Pope Potter seemed to have forgotten him. Both hands clasped, He stood wordless in the middle of the pool his robe now appearing to be spectrally clean in the faded evening, rigid in the ecstasy of the revelation which had been vouchsafed him alone after so long, after so very long.

"Like that statue which was really a fountain," Kip whispered to himself, remembering a picture in one of his aunt's books about some old palace in France. *Maybe, if he waited, the old man too would begin to spout water!* The thought made him smile.

Suddenly it seemed momentarily lighter as it often does shortly before real darkness sets in and Kip, disliking the idea of a long walk in the dark, struggling to squeeze still-damp feet into sneakers which seemed too tight these days, broke a lace in his impatience to be gone. Snatching the boater onto his head he set off at a trot.

Pope Potter, stirred by the sound of his departure, came slowly out of the water and stood gazing at the tree under which the boy had been dressing. The great black dog, which had been lying, watching, joined him, silently as if it were a malign spirit manifesting itself from Hell.

As soon as Kip saw the lights in the school he slowed. There was still a very faint touch of light in the sky away in the west although the stars were invisible against the half-blackness. He had begun to feel apprehensive. The business at Splash-Puddle now seemed oddly unsettling rather than awesome. The spell cast in that moment of silence before the old man had poured water over his head had vanished. "Pope Potter is just plain *barmy,*" he said aloud as if to convince himself. Stopping to recover his breath he put his hands on his hips, "My knife!" The sheath was empty.

Twice on the run back he'd slipped, once gone sprawling and rolling down a bank. It must have been be there. He half-turned. No point! Too dark now in the forest, which lay black, threatening behind him. He was annoyed at his carelessness. Not only had it seemed to him that it meant people thought he was growing up, but Young Miss Parroty was one of those people who always inquired about the presents they gave you. "How's the knife, Kip, dear?" she'd be sure to ask before turning to any adult nearby, "I gave him a lovely knife for his birthday, didn't I, Kip?" and he would be expected to thank her all over again.

It was unlikely that any of the other boys would keep it even if they found it. Anyhow the bank down which he had slipped was a short-cut of his own devising. Rust? No not in this drought. He had nothing to worry about; he'd recover it in the morning as soon as it was light, well before anyone else was likely to be about.

He arrived just in time for supper during which he referred sketchily to the incident at Splash-Puddle. "That dotty old man

wanted us to play some sort of game pouring water over me…
an' I think he wanted *me* to do the same over him but I was gettin'
cold. Anyway he was too tall. An' I di'n't want to miss supper!"

Pennery listened, initially with amused interest, then with
increasing unease. He had been curious about Pope Potter
who had first made an appearance with his tricycle-borne
altar-harmonium at least a decade before his own arrival. He
suspected the old man was somehow descended from one of
the fanatical religious families that had settled Salter's Creek at
the time of the gold rush.

"You couldn't have had very much of a bathe with Pope
Potter in there with you," Pennery responded more lightly and
casually than instinct warned him he ought to feel, although,
in truth, Kip seemed to have suffered no actual harm. "But I
shouldn't make a particular buddy of Pope Potter." Pennery
believed in letting sleeping dogs lie. Had he pressed for more
details of the encounter, as Patterson certainly would have done,
he would have been very greatly concerned.

"Is he 'raving mad', Mr Pennery? That's what the others say."

"Hardly that, though of course he does rave, especially on
Sundays in the Square as you've probably heard. Just a little
'touched' I supposed we might say."

"Yee-es…I s'pose it's not as if he goes round bashin' people
over the head or anything."

"No. At least I've never heard of any violence." He considered
again what the boy had told him. "No, I don't think he's
dangerous, probably lonely as much as anything."

"And mad of course."

"A *little* mad perhaps."

"He smelled pretty bad."

Pennery laughed out loud. "I bet he did. Reckon that must
have been his first bath for a long time."

"Do you think it was his bath-night? I mean perhaps once

a year or something. I read in one of your books that some religions believe in…total *imm*…something…sort of bathing."

"Total immersion is the word you want." On the point of explaining that it was a form of baptism he decided to imply something less significant, lighter with more innocuous, "Wouldn't surprise me, Kip if that was the first bath he's *ever* taken."

"Mmmm…'cept when he got wet, the stink was even worse. I could smell it even up on the bank when I got out."

Meal finished, plates washed, the conversation ended, Pennery had some work to prepare for the following day. Kip felt weary but could not get to sleep. His precious knife must have slipped out of its sheath when he slid down that bank. He *must* find it before he came face to face with Young Miss Parroty. She was quite often at the school-house with her elder sister who arranged for weekly laundry to go to Mr Soong and prepared supper for them on most evenings. Although it was left in the oven or, during the hot weather, as a collation in the cold-cupboard, he sometimes encountered the two sisters as they were leaving. If there wasn't time to search properly first thing in the morning, he'd go back again directly school finished. He might never have dropped off to sleep again had he known that he was to spend most of his spare time looking for it without any success at all.

10

It was Randall himself who noticed the first fire. By sheer chance he glanced out of his bedroom window and spotted a thin, wavering column turning orange like the great globe of the full moon, which most fortunately happened to be in the one spot which made the smoke visible.

Through his night-glasses he took a bearing, estimating the distance on a very large scale map on the wall of the room he used as his home office. It appeared to be between three and five miles away; he measured out a line onto the talc which had been gridded into zones for fire-fighting purposes and drew a tentative circle with a red chinagraph pencil. From a rack of pigeonholes, each numbered to correspond with one of the zones marked on the wall-map, he selected a detailed sketch-map, sliding it into a slipcase which he hung round his neck. The telephone operator he had alerted had already roused the rest of the stand-by team for that night. He had also telephoned Loxton and Special Constable Oates telling them in what direction they would be going. From a locked drawer he took the ex-army Verey pistol to alert more help if needed but then, remembering the inflammable state of the forest, knew he dared not risk firing it, whatever happened, and replaced it. If necessary one of them would go back to summon reinforcements although as far as he could estimate the fire seemed quite small.

Several cars were waiting in a loose half-circle outside the shed which housed the emergency vehicle heavy with haulage tackle, equipped with floodlight and siren.

"Smoke thick enough to be seen for five miles, but no glow at all. We may just dowse it in time to prevent a blaze spreading."

"Where is it?" a soft voice called from a station-waggon with its engine running.

"Somewhere in Z5, probably the north-east corner."

"Christ!" muttered another voice in the dimness.

"That's well off the road!" A different, deeper, voice.

"But there is a track most of the way," encouraged a third. "All the way if we push it, but only high-clearance cars'll make it."

There was a muttering as one of the vehicles emptied itself. "Can we come with you, Dill?" croaked a whisky voice, which was unfair; Lammerton was a fanatical teetotaller. "Don't reckon my bus'll make it, if it's really rough, I've had the sump off it twice this year already." Three more men squeezed beside and behind Randall and the vehicle lurched heavily.

They were not far from the schoolhouse and Pennery, not on call that evening, and who had been still working came to the door, open because of the heat. "Is it far?"

"Four or five miles," a voice shouted back as they sped past to collect another of the team standing ready by the road. They were stopped at The Manse by a figure waving a torch.

"Hell-*lo* Patterson, welcome back on the roster. Joyce? OK now is she?"

"Better anyhow. At least I feel I can now leave her at night occasionally if need be. But," he added with meaningful emphasis, "only in the cause of my *public duty*, you understand."

Randall understood the implication: "When she's really right, you must both come down and have supper with us!"

Patterson permitted himself a self-congratulatory smile in

the dark. He disapproved of hospitality not being returned. On principle. Patterson justified all his objections 'on principle'.

Already most of them were sweating in the confined space of the cars although all windows were open. Someone with a harsh voice said thoughtfully, "Z5 north-east? Mmmmm. You know that'd be about Splash-Puddle. Fortunately that track's much better now than it used to be. I met that nut Pope Potter there some days ago. Tricycle and all!"

"We used to bathe there as kids," came another older voice. "I remember we'd stay there quite late after school sometimes… even light a fire…cook 'dogs and…" His voice trailed off as he realised the implication of what had begun as a light-hearted reminiscence.

"Lighting fires? Hope your summers then were wetter than ours today," Randall called over his shoulder.

"If it's those kids again," the harsh voice interrupted on, "by Chr… sorry Padre… I'll be at that school insisting their arrases are tanned till they're raw. If Pennery won't, I'll thrash'm'all myself!"

"I don't think it's likely it's anything to do with the boys," Randall interposed. "Not after the Smokers Club. Anyhow it's no use getting worked up now. We're not even sure it is Splash-Puddle." He paused: "Of course it may be that old coot Potter if he was there."

"He never lights a fire, never cooks."

"Never? Howdj'know that?"

"Heard him say so. Eats only vegetables, fruit…an' bread when he c'n scrounge it. Drinks only cold water. No, he's safer in the woods than most." The anonymous speaker relapsed into silence.

The source of the smoke did indeed turned out to be Splash-Puddle; it poured out and up through the leaves of an enormous pile of very green wood stacked in the middle of the clearing.

At the edge of the smouldering conflagration lay a charred fragment of rag stinking of paraffin.

"Christ," said the blaspheming voice again, "Jes-*us C-er-rist*, fancy this little lot. Only wanted to burn down the whole fu… *unny* forest," he finished skilfully remembering Patterson's presence just in time.

"I suppose it *could* be the boys. A bathing club or something… . Cooking sausages?" came a more emollient contribution.

"This isn't for cooking it looks…well…deliberate…" Special Constable Oates interrupted, "as if we were meant to notice it… the smoke I mean…in order to drag us out at night," he ended almost apologetically for suggesting such a juvenile motive.

"Wouldn't put even that past *some* boys these days," snapped Patterson, implying he could think of at least one.

"Let's get it out anyhow," muttered Randall. They set about dismantling smouldering pile methodically dowsing it with water pumped from the nearby pool, throwing any still-glowing embers into the water, where they floated, hissing for a time before disappearing into the bowels of the earth.

"Perhaps the boys got their clothes wet and wanted to dry them," Patterson persisted, his suspicion that children were the culprits becoming a conviction.

It irritated Randall. "No *evidence!*"

Owens, one of the partners in the saw mill near the river observed sarcastically, "For drying clothes this would be about as much use as kissing 'em dry! They'd be better running home wearing 'em. It's four miles on foot even taking short cuts, they'd be dry long before they got home."

"Anyway," reasoned a mild voice, "they wouldn't have *swum* in their clothes. They swim in the buff, like we all did and what's more our kids aren't so dumb as to leave a fire burning even if they lit one."

"It is as if whoever it was wants to get us all out here at an inconvenient time as you suggested, Oates," Randall mused thoughtfully. "*Could* it be just as a joke I wonder?"

"A very *bad* joke," Patterson spat.

"What I mean…" Randall pursed his lips, "is…"

"Boys like *bad* jokes," Patterson insisted loudly.

"What I mean is," Randall continued, pointedly ignoring Patterson and turning round to them, "what I'm getting at is that I don't think this fire would have flared up. Ever. It's all green wood. Just a smoker. To attract attention as Oates says. Anyone who wants to set the forest on fire only needs gather some dry brushwood to drop a match."

"The oddest thing is," put in the saw-mill man, "that it's built out of *holly*." Greeted by uncomprehending silence, he ploughed on, "What I mean to says is that holly would have had to have been deliberately brought here. Nothing like it within a dozen miles. The nearest clump I know is in Z2 and that's a pretty small bush."

"But may there not be some unknown sources?" Patterson interrupted. "Can you be sure that *you* know *all* the possibilities?"

"No, no can't say that I could swear to it, but some of these branches are far bigger than you'd find casually, needed a big saw." He paused: "An' I jus' can't see *kids*…" The fact that Owen's speciality was selecting trees for the saw mill spoke volumes, as did his thirty years tracking down particular rare woods for special orders.

"We might," said Randall, "use the spotlight and our torches to see if the bastard, whoever he is, has left any clues." He intended it to lighten the atmosphere, but they took him up on it seriously. Lamps and torches slowly scanned the ground.

"Ah-*ha!*" Patterson held something up in the air. "A broken lace…about two inches long from a boy's sneaker *and* it includes the metal tag." He sounded triumphant. "We can parade all the boys when they're back in school and see who's got a broken lace, or even a new one, and we'll have the culprit."

"I'd hate to disillusion you, Patterson," Randall's voice came gently from behind his lamp, "but even if we find it *did* belong to one of them, there's no reason why they shouldn't have come here to bathe days ago. Could even have been from last year."

In the spotlight Patterson looked stubbornly crestfallen, "You mean *I'm* not a very good detective!" Indicating that he still believed the shoelace was a vital clue, "You asked for *evidence* and here it is and the tag's not rusted," he persisted mulishly, "so it can't have been there all last winter."

Just before they left, Randall, standing by the tree where Kip Harrison had undressed, saw something gleaming. He bent down and picked up a small medicine bottle. It stank of paraffin. They all crowded round. "No doubt now about it being deliberate!"

"Finger prints?" queried an excited voice from the dark, but they could see smears on the glass where it had been wrapped in rag, presumably to prevent it breaking.

"Perhaps the bottle is traceable," Patterson began, but even as he said it he knew it was the sort of small medicine bottle to be found in almost every bathroom cabinet. They switched out most of the torches and began to move off. The sky was already lightening with the first glimmers of a new day.

Dawn was well advanced when they got back to Salter's Creek and dispersed. Randall's wife was waiting for him with coffee.

"Out?" she enquired. "Without too much trouble?"

"Out this time. Next time we may not be so lucky."

"Perhaps there won't be a next time."

"There will, unless we have rain. What news of the big one?" He referred to what newspapers and radio news flashes had already christened The Great Blaze which they now knew had started far to the west on the day of the ants.

"Spreading, according to the news." Pouring him more coffee, she had been listening to the radio throughout the time he was absent. "Eating its way east they say."

"Lucky there's no wind." He took a sip of coffee, then thoughtfully added, "Jumped the main road?"

"Yes, that's right, it has. Impassable ninety miles west of us according to the bulletin. Then it always is with a big one. Why so gloomy, Dill?"

"Somebody may be trying to set the forest on fire, although…" He paused. "It's…well it's almost as if we're being sent some sort of message." He told her of the green wood.

"From what you say, could be it's just a prank. Some boy who got well tanned over that Smokers Club business. Now he's older, thought he'd get his own back. Probably in the bushes watching you all the time."

"I'd've given him something to remember if I'd spotted him! But the Smokers Club was what…three years ago?"

"Some who got a real thrashing from their fathers getting their own back? If there's more than one, collecting wood's no problem. And who's going to notice a saw missing for a couple of hours? Now they've had their fun dragging you all out that'll be the end of it."

Her conviction that it was, as Patterson had insisted, nothing but a very bad joke, a one-off hoax, though a dangerous one, soothed him into the deep slumber of those whose hard work has earned them a just reward. Sleep might not have come so quickly had he known that far from being the end, the incident at Splash-Puddle was only the beginning.

Woken by blaring by sirens and hooters as the squad had set off, Kip had rushed to the window watching until their headlights were swallowed up in the trees; whenever the emergency group on duty set off, there was always the same swooping warning-siren blare that made his stomach turn over.

Tonight it was even worse: now wide awake he was wondering with increasing anxiety how soon he would find his knife. Where *exactly* had he lost it? He'd not found it when he'd crept out early before breakfast and, after he'd finished helping Pennery with a few domestic chores, he had spent the rest of the day looking for it until it was too dark to see. He'd been so very certain it had fallen out of its sheath somewhere near the bank down which he'd slipped. The undergrowth was so thick and tangled that he had searched the area three times without success.

How would he ever face Young Miss Parroty? He'd do his best to avoid her and leave the sheath beneath his socks in a drawer, hoping that if she did happen to notice he wasn't wearing it she'd assume he wanted to keep it pristine, without having to explain. Anyway, he comforted himself, he'd *surely* find it tomorrow which was Saturday (or was it tomorrow already?) when he'd have all the time in the world.

However, he did not find it where he had tripped and fallen although he spent all weekend in that area. He had a disinclination to search the clearing at Splash-Puddle because in the first place he was convinced that he'd had it on his belt when he'd left. Furthermore now, in view of the gossip suggesting the green-wood fire had been a dangerous hoax on the part of one or more of the Smokers Club culprits, it seemed politic to avoid associating himself with Splash-Puddle, let alone advertising his presence there the very day before the mysterious fire. He began to regret that he had mentioned the incident even to Pennery, although now he thought about it, the schoolmaster's reaction to his account of their Splash-Puddle encounter had not quite been what he had expected, almost as though Pennery had been warning him, though against quite what he was uncertain. Nonetheless it strengthened an instinctive underlying reluctance to chance another encounter with Pope Potter.

11

i

It was not so much that the heatwave disappeared – no dramatic change, no showers of rain – but that it became so much the norm that everyone got used to it. The pall of smoke from The Great Blaze to the west had become part of the sky and *The Sentinel* made great play of the green-wood fire at Splash-Puddle, in consequence the fire-watch tower, replete with three loudspeakers, was now manned for an hour at dawn, midday and from dusk into the late hours.

Leonard Patterson made his regular visit the very morning school restarted. Still convinced that the shoe-lace clue would provide the answer, he abandoned his timetabled Bible lesson.

"The Splash-Puddle fire-raiser left a clue at the scene," he announced dramatically. "The culprit," and, looking slowly round the room, making it clear *he* knew it was one of *them*, "left behind a piece of evidence. Which *I* found," he concluded with scarcely concealed triumph. Anxious to compare the end of the lace he had recovered with laces in the shoes of the boys in front of him, Patterson took the grubby white-grey 'evidence' from his pocket with a melodramatic gesture. Had he been less complacent, more astute, and waited to see who stirred uncomfortably at his disclosure, he might have noticed Kip stiffen and blanch momentarily. "If you are wearing sneakers bought from Parrotys come out here." A dozen boys of all ages from nine to thirteen, including Kip, shuffled sheepishly to the front of the class.

"Now," said Patterson triumphantly, "we'll see who has a new lace. Or a broken one!" Kip knew the broken lace must be his, he remembered it parting when he was tugging on his shoes as he hurried to get back before it got too dark. However, when dressing the following morning he had broken the other lace and, rather than ask for new he had merely taken worn laces from an old pair which he had outgrown.

Patterson's inspection revealed not a single new lace, furthermore only Kip and Calum McKay, son of the man who had written the inflammatory Smokers Club letter to *The Sentinel,* had unbroken laces and they were very obviously not new. Faced with ten suspects, each of whom was able to explain exactly what he was doing for the three or four hours on the evening in question – the older ones cheekily implying that if Patterson did not believe *them* he could go and check with their parents. Stubbornly refusing to relinquish his investigative role, he remarked angrily, "This lace was not the only clue," without revealing he was referring to the bottle stinking of paraffin. Kip was even more worried. True, Patterson did not know that the broken shoelace was his, but had they also found his knife there? Nobody yet knew he'd lost it. He hadn't bothered to mention it to Pennery because, so certain had he been that he knew where he'd dropped it, it didn't seem as if it was really lost at all.

That evening he went searching once more. Returning as it

was getting dark, having spent further fruitless hours, he almost collided with 'Mayor' Loxton (whose garden was his pride and joy) out collecting a particular moisture-retaining moss which remained damp even in the hottest weather. He was intending to use it to surround some much-cherished delicate plants suffering from days of fierce sun, however much he watered them early each morning and evening. Kip offered to carry the dripping bundle.

Loxton took the opportunity to ask again how he was getting on at the schoolhouse and was once more impressed as much by Kip's uninhibitedly positive response as by the very obvious evidence that Pennery's ward was bursting with health.

Exactly a week to the day after the Splash-Puddle conflagration, the fire squad rushed out on another evening call. The observer on duty in the fire-tower reported smoke rising from a spot in the forest well north of Splash-Puddle. When Randall and his squad eventually arrived at the reference given, they once again found carefully stacked holly branches pouring thick smoke into the night air. Loxton, Patterson and Pennery were not on call that particular evening but it so happened that Rogerson was because he happened to live not far from the probable site and Randall had telephoned him. He was caustic about Patterson's efforts to trace the 'firebug' which his son had related; the picture of Patterson faced by ten small suspects with broken laces, all of whom were clearly blameless, briefly lightened the atmosphere. One of Rogerson's motives in telling the tale, was to make it quite clear that *his* son (one of the original Smokers Club offenders) had not only a complete set of laces, but had been with his father stooking hay all day even though it was Sunday, "preferring honest hard work, sensible laddie that he is, to listening to sermons in the company of his mother and two sisters".

Fire well and truly out, they walked wearily to their vehicles, getting back just in time to learn that a second fire had been reported in another direction. The reserve squad, which did include Loxton, Pennery and Patterson, was preparing to set out. Tired as he was, Randall joined them and it was almost midnight before they conquered the second fire. It too was obviously deliberate and also of green wood but, although it was clearly another attempt to attract attention, by the time they reached it there were visible flames and drifting sparks had already set tinder-dry undergrowth smouldering.

"Near thing that," murmured Randall, "a very near thing!" speaking to himself, but noticing the others were listening and nodding. "We can all see that had this one got out of hand…I mean although even if it was only meant to cause smoke…a joke…a hoax…we were lucky to get here in time to…"

"Hoax?" a voice enquired.

"*Joke!*" another echoed.

"If it's meant as a joke," exclaimed a young plump man, who was in fact Owen's son and, like his father, worked with the saw mill, "then it's a pretty elaborate joke for kids."

"Elaborate? *Criminal!* I don't care if they *are* children," snapped Patterson taking off his spectacles leaving pale circles on his soot-begrimed face.

"We don't know that, Patterson," Loxton pointed out. "I can't believe *kids* could do this…it's so…organised."

Pulling his spectacles back on, Patterson, still irritated by Loxton's disinclination to repair the choir balcony, sensitive to the possibility that the debacle over the supposed clue of the broken lace had made him look ridiculous and aware that Pennery was listening, exploded. "Well I'll be astonished if what lies at the bottom of it doesn't turn out to be *sheer ill-discipline,*" clearly implying *at the school* as he stomped back towards the vehicles.

Half an hour after they returned, Randall had to rouse the first squad again. Somebody on his way home very late after visiting friends in Salter's Creek, rang in to report a pall of smoke across the road from an almost inaccessible area and they had finally to hack their way through the last fifty yards of thick dry undergrowth to find another greenly smoking 'hoax'. Fortunately on this occasion they arrived just as it was developing into a far more dangerous blaze, up-currents of hot air lifting sparks, and even small glowing embers, high in the air towards even more flammable fallen trees. By the time it was completely dowsed their faces were black, sticky with soot.

"Very lucky to find *that* one in time," said an anonymous voice from the dark as they drove wearily back hardly speaking, dog-tired. Randall, having attended all three, was filthy, sweat had carved white lines through the grime on his face which showed the strain he felt himself under. They arrived as dawn was already touching the eastern sky.

Still in his filthy clothes, he sat drinking his wife's hot coffee gazing intently and thoughtfully at the wall map. Edith Randall was too wise to ask what was worrying him. Studying the map with even greater concentration, he made a large dot with a red marker, then, taking up a pair of dividers, measured distances, checked the measurements and drew three red circles numbering them 1, 2, 3. Frowning, he took another careful measurement and this time drew in green another circle surrounding a large question mark. He peered at the map again, looked at his watch, then took his binoculars to the porch.

It was still dark in the west with that brief lack of moon and starlight characteristic of the final half-hour before the sun comes up. He scanned very carefully for several minutes. Putting down the binoculars, he studied the wall map one last time and reached for the phone.

Both squads, lethargic, weary, ill-tempered, reassembled with a promptness which did them credit. When they reached the fire it was evident that it had been lit barely half an hour before they arrived, and took only minutes to dis-assemble the green wood and sappy plantain leaves, by which time it was quite light. They found no evidences of the culprit. Whoever it was had been very careful.

"Only just missed him," Randall mused.

"Not even a broken shoelace this time," somebody sniped at Patterson but they were all far too tired for it even to raise a smile.

"When did you see this one?"

"Was it reported in?" somebody else asked as they tramped back to the transport. "How did we know where it was?"

"Luck," Randall muttered indistinctly. "Thought I'd have another look around before I turned in."

"Pretty lucky to spot it. The smoke was thin."

"Dawn, you know," Randall said enigmatically, enough to indicate he wanted no further discussion.

They gathered listlessly in the centre of the road before moving off. The worst part of fire-fighting was that you could never smoke on the job. Back in Salter's Creek, Pennery announced that he'd never make the classroom before midday. Asking the others to spread the news, he pinned a notice to on the schoolroom door saying that classes would begin in the afternoon and, leaving another note for Kip, went to bed where he fell asleep the moment his head touched the pillow.

Randall, apprehensively untired, found Edith still up and they sat drinking yet more coffee on the veranda which was comfortably cool.

"Where was it this time, Dill?"

"You oughtn't to wait up for me." She looked tired and drawn in the morning light.

"Would you like me to go to bed when you're out?" Looking

at him affectionately, "Really?"

"It's nice you're here when I get back. Always with hot coffee. But that's just me being selfish. There's no need for two of to have our rest ruined." He put his hand over hers.

"But, Dill, I like waiting up makes me feel part of it. And there might be messages on the phone. Anyhow, I couldn't sleep if I knew you were out there fighting a forest fire..."

Odd, he reflected how, after so many years of married life, he was more in love with her than ever. When they married, he had been fond of her but, he now realised, he hadn't been in love. Guiltily he recalled that he had married her mainly because he knew she loved him and he'd not the courage to disappoint her. He gave her hand a squeeze.

"Anyhow, Dill dear, where was it this time?"

"Come, I'll show you." He took her inside to the map.

He indicated the three red circles marked 1, 2, 3. "It was there, the green one." He rubbed out the question mark and put 4 in red. Then with a straight rule drew a line upper and lower red circles 1 and 3 and another from left to right joining red circle 2 to the green circle which bisected the first line exactly where the dot had been placed.

"How did you hear of it, dear? It's a long way off. Or did you spot it through the binoculars?"

"No. That's the point, I *didn't* spot it. There was no smoke to see."

"Did Henry get a phone call? Nobody rang here!"

"There was no phone call."

"What did you do...guess?"

"Not a *guess*." He paused and said quietly, "I *predicted* it." He paused again. "I knew where the next one would be – approximately."

She returned his stare, puzzled.

"Look, Edith," placing the dividers on the red dot in the

centre of the cross. "This," indicating the green circle, "was where we found the last fire we attended tonight and this," indicating the large central red dot, "is Splash-Puddle."

"Why, they're all about the same distance…"

"Exactly, Splash-Puddle – site of the first fire – is ringed by those we attended to night. And notice this—" He stabbed the red rings he had added that evening. He enunciated carefully, "One *North* – Two *South* – Three *West* so Four had to be…" He put his finger on the green circle with the question mark.

"East! Of course! I have got a clever husband." She put an arm round his waist.

"If I'd only tumbled to it whilst we were dealing with the third fire, we might have caught the firebug as he was lighting the fourth."

"It couldn't be coincidence I suppose…" Her voice died away as he shook his head.

"North, South, West, And now East? Can't be anything but a deliberate plan."

"All green fires? Like the one last Sunday?" He nodded. "Well at least if it *is* only an elaborate *joke*…" she began doubtfully. "But who…?"

"Perhaps Patterson's on the right lines, after all Splash-Puddle was where the Smokers Club met."

"But why, Dill?"

"Twisting our tails? Getting us all up at night?"

"They'd have to be pretty well-organised, Dill, even the oldest are only what? Thirteen? Fourteen? And it would have to be several of them, wouldn't it? I mean tonight there were four fires and to build and light them in just a few hours…"

"I take the point, Edith, but it just could be one boy. After all since that first one at Splash-Puddle there's been plenty of time all week to build tonight's fires. Only needs one to nip round lighting them." He pointed to the number 4, ringed in green. "We'd probably have caught him here, at the last one, had I been quicker on the uptake."

"But what is he...are they...getting out of it apart from the feeling that he's getting his own back?"

"That's just it, I don't know..." Suddenly a look of enlightenment crossed his face, "Unless, of course they want a half-day!"

"A *half-day*, Dill?"

"If Pennery's out on one of these late night alarms, then they get the morning off so he can sleep in. The weekly roster is posted in *The Sentinel*, so they know when he's on call."

"They must realise the fire danger!"

"Remember how the Smokers Club culprits were punished? Some of their fathers were well...Pennery told me one or two of the boys really could only *stand* at their desks the next day."

"But they're nice kids," she said thoughtfully. "They really are, Dill, we're very lucky here in that we don't have these problem children I've read about."

"We haven't...at least...not until now, Edith. But you're right, we've always known them...since they were born..." He hesitated: "Most of them anyway." The same unspoken thought was in both minds *What did they know of Kip's background before he came to live with his great aunt?* Even as the words formed in his head, he realised that, if the reason for the fires was to bring about a half-holiday, then it would hardly be Kip who was responsible. Not only was he living with the schoolmaster but he quite evidently enjoyed what school offered.

"I hope you're right, Edith. But if it *is* one of the smokers doing it for a lark – he'll know he can't continue dragging holly across the forest without somebody spotting him – and if he starts to make fires out of dry wood..." That was the fear that nagged him constantly, that worried him most. On each occasion so far they'd got there in time only because the fire had not been intended to do more than produce smoke. If somebody set a really good fire going they'd be defeated long before they got to it. With the menace of The Great Blaze to the west of them, it was like fighting an unseen insurgent enemy.

"Perhaps Pennery should have made more fuss about the smoking after all." Edith Randall pursed her lips. "I wonder if he was too easy on them. They say it was because of young Kip Harrison being his ward and…"

"That's just gossip, Edith." He was reminded of Patterson's determination to blame the boys. "Even spiteful gossip." He patted her hand, "Inaccurate too. People seem to overlook the fact that, at the time of the Smokers Club, Pennery was not Kip's guardian, merely his schoolmaster. They have either forgotten or…" Patterson's accusations came to mind, "…choose not to remember that Kip Harrison was living with his aunt."

"I just wasn't thinking," she admitted guiltily. "You're quite right, Dill. Of course at the time of the Smokers Club the boy had been here barely three months…scarcely eight years old, recovering from the crash which killed both his parents."

"Moreover," Randall added, "Pennery has always been quite certain that Kip was never one of the smokers…Gossip! Tittle-tattle! Malicious in some quarters I begin to suspect."

"But perhaps he resents Leonard for trying to ensure he should be punished for his Sunday 'truancy' – Patterson would be amongst those called out at night."

"In all honesty, Edith can you see the open and forthcoming kid we've always enjoyed meeting deliberately setting and lighting *five* fires as a protest?" He drew a weary breath and drained his cup. "I'm quite sure Pennery'd stop Kip from doing anything stupid or dangerous. It's just not Pennery's way to beat his pupils on the slightest excuse, or indeed at all, unlike old 'Blastarse' Henry tells us about. The fact is, unusually for a schoolmaster perhaps, he declines to be judge and executioner… . At least that's what he said to me. I respect him for it, every community needs somebody like him."

Edith Randall's mind seemed suddenly very clear; awareness of the new day, perception of the nagging sense of urgency that was jading her husband sharpened her intuition. "That's just it! As Bella and I were saying the other night, though we didn't express it very well. What *Pennery* judges to be *wrong* or *right* may not be enough. Perhaps he's too tolerant by nature."

"For Salter's Creek?"

"Yes! That is no – not for *us*, but as the guardian for this particular boy."

"Don't you believe he'd stop Kip from doing anything stupid or dangerous?"

"Of course he would *if he noticed*, but perhaps he's just too… too *casual* to care properly for a child, especially one whose background we don't know."

"You think the Pattersons would have been better, that Kip would have been happier there?"

"Well to be honest I am not sure that the boy would have been as *happy* there as he seems to be with Pennery, but Patterson might have been a better *father* figure. It's almost as if Pennery were an indulgent elder brother. I'm quite sure, from what Leonard has said, that Joyce had set her heart on having the boy and he would take a firmer line don't you think, Dill? Know what the boy was up to and where he'd been."

"You're not *really* suggesting that Pennery never noticed Kip wasn't in bed and asleep before he left with us tonight and the boy was racing ahead us of lighting the fires?"

"No. I didn't mean that…though I suppose he might have done. They do say that children who lose their parents can be quite seriously disturbed."

"I must say," Randall interrupted almost laughing, "that I

have never seen, or met, a less disturbed kid in my life. And, as Loxton says, we're all responsible for looking after the boy. Every one of us here in Salter's Creek is his guardian."

"That's just it..." She frowned, then with a flash of insight, "Don't you see, Dill? When *everyone* is responsible then, in a crisis, it turns out no *one* person has taken responsibility because we all think he's the responsibility of somebody else. What I'm trying to say, Dill, is, that for some reason, Pennery doesn't seem willing to get himself *personally* involved enough in *anything* to be able to recognise a crisis if or when it arises." She paused. "There are moments when there has to be one *special* person. Somebody who offers a word of warning, gives good advice or even in the case of a child, just says, 'No!' Kip is only eleven, he needs somebody who, in the last resort, can make a decision which he will obey however unwelcome it may seem, because he accepts that the adult making it knows best – and, usually, secretly respects him or her for that very reason. A bond of affection is the best guarantee, the surest safety device so to speak, especially with children. Pennery is an excellent teacher but I sense somehow that he doesn't want to be emotionally tied."

"I'm not sure what you're getting at, Edith?"

"Well, look at him. We all *like* him, but he holds himself, oh I don't know...apart...remote. Do we even remember his Christian name? And," she added tellingly, "if we ever do, do we ever use it? He'll always be Pennery to us, or *Mr* Pennery to the children even to Kip who is his ward."

"I think it's Pennery's detachment that young Kip values most. He's reaching that sort of age when sometimes even loving friends can be a nuisance by interfering." Randall reflected on his own youth. "Though no doubt with the best of intentions!"

"With children of *any* age that sort of interference can be a safeguard. Especially when things aren't quite normal." She looked meaningfully at the map.

"We've had fires before of course. Most years."

"Like these? And don't let's forget The Great Blaze although it's still a long way off only needs a strong wind."

"No, of course you're right, Edith, never fires like these and, as you say, there's The Great Blaze over to the west. Do you really think we should do something about Kip and Pennery?"

"Perhaps not now, not immediately." Already her conviction of a few moments before had weakened. "No, what I'm trying to say is that the Pattersons, man *and wife*, might have been preferable but, as you say, Kip seems to be very happy with Pennery and after losing first his parents and now his aunt we mus'n't act in haste." She paused: "Anyhow at the moment Joyce is far from well and, Dill, I suspect it may be more than just heat-stroke."

"Nevertheless," Randall assured her, "I think I'll have a quiet word with Pennery tomorrow."

ii

"Why blame the *boys*," Pennery objected when Randall raised the matter the following day. "Why *these* boys? Look, there may be nutters, criminals, or even jokers, around, but it's quite unwarranted to suspect the boys just because of the smoking business which was years ago and no sign of any such foolish behaviour since then."

"*I* don't *suspect* them, Pennery, nevertheless I just think we should take every step to make sure that it really *isn't* just some kid wanting an extra half-day off school because you've been up all night."

"Well," Pennery laughed, "If omitting my name from the fire-roster is your solution, it suits me. I'd far rather feel awake enough to teach than fight fires. But if you do ever need all hands just ring me – better still," he suggested after a moment's thought, "why not put me on at the weekend for the present, Friday and Saturday when the school is in session and I can be back on call all the time when we're having a break?" It was a sensible solution. If Pennery were off the rota entirely it might encourage weary and suspicious minds to complain that the schoolmaster alone was being specially favoured although the whole crisis might well be the result of his failure to discipline his ward.

"I still think it's somewhere else you want to look, Dill. What about those mail robbers? If you hadn't recognised them when they stopped to fill up with petrol, they'd probably be still free. Didn't they swear they'd get revenge one day and I should think they're out on parole now, some of them anyway?"

Randall shook his head. "No, the two still alive have years to go. The two brothers *were* on parole but were both shot dead attempting to rob that bank in Ottawa. The last one died 'inside' two years ago."

"What about Pope Potter? He's mad enough for anything." Pennery had said nothing so far to anyone about the bizarre encounter between the old man and Kip at Splash-Puddle. Should he perhaps mention it to Randall now?

"The Pope's been around for a long time." *Longer than you, Pennery, was the implication.* "I can't imagine why he'd start on a caper like this now. Crazy I grant you but perfectly harmlessly preaching every Sunday to nobody but that damn dog."

"Lovers and madmen have such seething brains, Dill, they don't think like us." The quotation was lost on Randell, *was Pennery laughing at him?*

At that moment Kip trotted briskly into the room but then, seeing Randall, stopped.

"Sorry, Mr Pennery, I've come for the bell."

"Kip rings the hand-bell for the end of our mid-day break,"

Pennery explained.

"How's Mr Pennery looking after you, Kip?" Randall said lightly enough, but with his wife's remarks the night before still in mind. Something in his tone put Kip on guard.

"Oh! Oh, ah jus' fine, Mr Randall." *Perhaps they really had found his knife!* "I like it here." *Was he about to be asked if he had been anywhere near Splash-Puddle?* "Mus'ring th'bell," before dashing out, clanging it vigorously until there was a mumble of voices and shuffling feet as the boys came back inside.

Randall, having heard for himself the boy express his satisfaction at the present living arrangement, turned back to Pennery. "The Pope's certainly an old nutter, but he's a harmless old nutter. Furthermore," Randall smiled "apart from our Creek, he's the only real claim to fame we've got! As I say, he turned up here twenty years ago and there've been no *mysterious* fires until this year. Not as if he'd only appeared recently…as if he were a newcomer for instance…" *Kip Harrison was a newcomer* hung unspoken in the air. The clanging stopped. *Had the boy looked slightly apprehensive when he'd addressed him just now? Guilty conscience?* Turning round towards the door, "By the way, Kip, have you…?" He realised the bell had been slipped back onto its shelf whilst he was speaking to Pennery; rising noise from the Big Schoolroom carried the schoolmaster off to quell it.

The more Randall thought about it, the more he had had to admit that his own suspicion was founded on nothing more than Patterson's inference that Kip's Sunday 'truancy' was due entirely to Pennery's refusal to discipline the boy appropriately. Could it really be that, as Edith suggested, Kip so deeply resented Patterson's demand that Pennery should beat him for missing church that he (a boy of what, eleven wasn't it?) would go to the lengths of building and setting alight five fires out in the forest just to annoy his tormentor? Was she right to wonder whether the loss, first of his parents and then his great aunt had unbalanced the youngster in some way?

Had Kip been still present, he would have at least asked if he had been to Splash-Puddle recently. That was where the first fire had been set and why Patterson, having found his so-called 'clue', had first propounded the notion that boys, or *a boy* was responsible. Had the Minister already had Kip in mind when he said that? Randall realised he ought to have organised a further search of the clearing in daylight the following morning. Far too late now, of course. Was Edith right? Perhaps a firmer hand might be the way ahead...Kip under the Minister's eye? Even as he considered this he had to admit that he himself at Kip's age would not have welcomed the intrusive supervision inevitable under Patterson's guardianship. Furthermore, if Kip Harrison were the firebug, harbouring a grievance because of Patterson's insistence he should be punished for his 'truancy,' he'd surely want to burn down Patterson's church! The thought made him smile, at least in that case they would be spared a sermon for a few weeks.

Randall and Edith had done Pennery something of an injustice when, like Patterson, they assumed he took little notice of what Kip did in his spare time, or where he went. In fact, on the evening after the first fire at Splash-Puddle, he had again asked Kip about his encounter with Pope Potter. "I wonder whether perhaps you had noticed anything. A pile of wood for instance? It seems that it was holly which had to have been brought some distance."

Kip shook his head.

"A bottle of paraffin?"

"No, Mr Pennery." Kip shook his head more vigorously. "I'd've noticed something as big as a pile of wood, 'spesh'ly holly 'cos I've never seen any holly growing at Splash-Puddle...

or anywhere…or a bottle…I'd've noticed *that*. Splash-Puddle was jus' like it always is, nothin' 'cept the grass, the rock an' the water. An' his tricycle of course."

"You say he poured water over you?" Pennery paused, wondering how to phrase it casually, "He didn't…touch you?"

"Oh yes. It was funny. He sort of stroked me."

"*Stroked* you!" Pennery interjected, startled, then deliberately more calmly, "Er…*stroked* you?"

"Yes, an' he looked a long time at my hands, 'spesh'ly the scars.'

Pennery had heard from old Miss Harrison that Kip, asleep in the back of the car when the smash occurred, had his hands badly cut by a shattered window as a courageous passing motorist dragged him barely conscious to the side of the road only minutes before the car and the vast vehicle which had been at fault burst into flames.

"And that was it?"

"Oh no, all the rest of me too. He hesitated. "Y'know, Mr Pennery, it was as if…" it came to him suddenly, "…as if he was making sure that I was *really* there with him…in Splash-Puddle." He paused thoughtfully, "An' not some sort of ghost… . Then he knelt down and touched my feet even though they were in the water." Kip wriggled awkwardly. "Don't know why but I…I tol' him 'bout the garden fork…" Kicking off one of his sneakers, he pointed to the circular scar, "See," kicking of the other, "both feet. It was when I was four…" whispering, "I was pretendin'…pretend*ing* …to be a frog…an'…I sort of hopped… jus' as my dad…" Embarrassed by confessing to such childish fantasy, he lapsed into silence.

"That was all?" Moved by the intimacy of the revelation, Pennery asked quietly and carefully, "Just stroked you and touched your feet? Were you frightened, Kip?"

"No. He didn't hurt me. 'S'funny, 'though he's got big thick fingers, they're so soft I could hardly feel them…" The boy thought again. "Soun's silly but y'know Mr Pennery, it was if he thought *I* was his *son*. As if he'd sort of *lost* his real son."

"And then?"

"Then it was jus' that business with pourin' water. An' I was feeling cold an' got out and put on my clothes which I'd left under the tree." He stopped. ***The tree!*** *Of course that was where he'd stuck the knife.* What a relief! He'd go after school and recover it.

Kip in bed and asleep, Pennery reviewed what he had learned: an old man stroking a boy standing naked in a remote forest pool, reciting what sounded, from Kip's faltering recall, almost Biblical words. Although the boy seemed completely unfazed by his encounter, indeed more amused than worried, Kip *was* only eleven and he, Pennery, was, however reluctantly, currently responsible for the boy's welfare. Not only must he impress on Kip that he should avoid any further contact with Pope Potter, he must ensure that in no circumstances should the boy ever again find himself alone with the old man either casually or accidentally. Pope Potter could no longer be ignored as the harmlessly eccentric preacher the community had hitherto tolerated with amusement. His behaviour seemed all at once not only more unpredictable, but distinctly sinister. Should he not warn the other children in the school? Loxton and Randall certainly had to be told precisely what had taken place at Splash-Puddle.

Of one thing he was now quite certain; although he was entirely happy for Kip to lodge with him in the schoolhouse, indeed he found the boy's company cheerfully refreshing, there was really no question of agreeing to become the *legal* guardian, let alone to adopt the boy: he had no intention ever again of accepting responsibility for the lives of others. However much he disliked Patterson, he had little doubt the Minister would prove a thoroughly conscientious foster-parent.

As soon as school finished Kip ran most of the way to Splash-Puddle, arriving hot and sweaty. He'd have time for a quick dip before leaving. He was glad to find no sign of Pope Potter, though some debris from the green-wood fire was evident, together with a few charred twigs too large to disappear into the rock fissure clustered at the side to the pool.

His knife was no longer in the tree.

He knew it was the right tree; when he looked closely, he could still see the slit where the blade had penetrated the bark. It must have fallen out! But although he searched the ground again and again there was no trace of it. He remembered Patterson's hint that they had another clue. *The fire-squad had found it!* Pennery had told him about finding a bottle but never mentioned a knife. Why not? *Because they were still trying to trace the owner who was the suspected firebug.* How long before somebody remembered to ask him about Young Miss Parroty's birthday present? All the other boys knew he had the knife and if Randall quizzed their fathers and older brothers about the whereabouts of *their* knives, no doubt one of them would mention Kip had one too, not least because they envied him.

If only he had mentioned the loss to Pennery on that first evening, but at the time he'd been so certain it was somewhere down the bank and that he'd be sure to find it the next day that it really hadn't seemed lost. Or even if he'd mentioned it last night, when explaining again about Pope Potter at Splash-Puddle. However, of course it wasn't until that last night that he'd finally remembered he'd stuck it in the tree...so it *still* hadn't been really *lost*. He walked back very slowly, unwillingly.

Was Mr Randall waiting there for him with 'Mayor' Loxton and Pennery? Would they believe his explanation? He arrived at the schoolhouse and found nobody except Pennery. The relief was enormous.

Although Pennery sat down with him, the table was set for one. "I'm not joining you because I'm bidden to the Loxton birthday party," adding lightly, "Hope there's no ants this time." No response. Kip seemed, very unusually for him, to be only toying with his food. "Something bothering you, Kip?" Silence. "These last few days you look like somebody whose lost a dollar and only found a cent."

"It's my knife," Kip burst out, "I've lost it an' Young Miss Parroty…I know she'll ask why I'm not wearing it…" He'd spoken before he realised it and now, to his shame, he found he had tears in his eyes. "Did they find it, Mr Patterson an'…?"

Pennery said gently, "Tell me about it," and listened without interrupting as Kip related the whole story including the days of searching. "So last night you finally remembered that it was in the tree…and you've been back this afternoon and…?"

Kip sniffing, "Not there. I thought Mr Patterson might have found it, he told us all there was another clue but didn't say what it was…"

Pennery shook his head, and laughed, "Nobody found a knife, not even Mr Patterson! No clues except that broken shoelace and the medicine bottle. You're absolutely certain there was no sign of your knife when you went back this afternoon?" Kip nodded. *Whew! At least they weren't going to suspect him of the fire!* Although momentarily puzzled by the boy's relieved reaction despite the fact his precious knife was *still* lost, Pennery had not the slightest doubt he had been told the truth.

Questioning them all as to their involvement at the time of the Smokers Club nonsense, long before he had become the boy's guardian, he had been struck by Kip's utter lack of guile.

This impression had been confirmed after Kip had come to live at the schoolhouse. He seemed, even in the smallest matters, to eschew any prevarication or evasiveness. In his first week, visibly plucking up his courage, he had appeared in the doorway on the morning after his aunt's funeral, head down.

"Last night I...last night I wet the bed."

Pennery had very gently lifted the boy's chin "Accidents happen, Kip, I admire you for telling me." A brief pause. "It happened to me first night I went away to school and I didn't dare tell anyone but of course Matron found out and that was much worse..." Even after all these years he was unable to continue.

"I'm very sorry, Mr Pennery, but when I was smaller my mother thought I might be an en...*en* something."

"Enuretic?"

"Yes! I'll wash the sheets an' turn the mattress an'...

"We'll do it together, Kip. The sheets can just go to the laundry when they're dry. And there's another mattress. We'll burn yours, it was pretty ancient anyway."

Pennery's matter-of-fact acceptance of the confession ensured there were no further 'accidents'. If he found such transparent honesty endearing in a boy of Kip's age, he had to confess he also found it more than a little daunting. He revised his provisional intention to let Loxton and Randall know that Kip had been at the scene of the first fire, it would only serve to bolster Patterson's suspicions which he was certain were unjustified: whoever was responsible for the fires he was quite sure it was not Kip Harrison. He might even offer to go with the boy to have another search for the lost knife.

12

After Pennery's arrival at Salter's Creek and his unpalatable discovery that the original 'Founders' had been spectacular fraudsters, Loxton's birthday had somehow been accorded the celebratory mantle of the Founders Day for which *The Sentinel* had agitated so vigorously. The last known McCutcheon having died on Vimy Ridge whilst serving with the 16th Battalion Canadian-Scottish, Loxton and the Parroty sisters were the only direct descendants of those responsible for developing the former trading post during the 'gold-rush' influx and who had stayed on thereafter. Thus his birthday party had, over time, become an occasion which anyone who was anybody expected to attend and, as Salter's Creek to a man (and woman) believed that everyone *was* somebody, virtually the entire population turned up, including Pennery who set off about the time Kip went to bed.

The only reason it was Loxton's rather than the Parroty sisters' birthday which had assumed the *rôle* was due solely to the fact that they had been born on the last day of November, by which time the entire area was usually deep in the first snowfall of winter. Sensitively and tactfully, Loxton accepted that the Parroty sisters were in effect co-hosts. This particular duty fell to Young Miss Parroty alone. Her sister who had become increasingly hard of hearing, the legacy of childhood measles, rarely attended social gatherings, rather to the relief, it must be admitted, of those who were daunted when the ear-trumpet, which she welded like an offence weapon, was thrust towards them.

This commitment did not however deflect Young Miss Parroty from organ practice. She was regular as clockwork. Each Tuesday at eight o'clock she went along to the church, opening the door with her own key, playing through her intended 'Impromptu' for the following Sunday. Salter's Creek was conservative regarding hymn tunes, steadfastly refusing to attempt any except those with which they were completely familiar. Hymns were not the subject of her organ practice evening because she could keep her fingers in trim for the twiddly bits in *Oh God our help in Ages past* and *Light of the World* at the regular Friday "run-through" for the choir.

In honour of the party she had donned her 'New Outfit' and this, together with her search for a mislaid glove, delayed her almost an hour. Like "Young", use of the term "New" was comparative. Purchased over fifty years earlier for her and her sister's joint twenty-first birthday, worn not more than twice a year at most, it still looked as if it had just come out of a shop although it would have been a theatrical costumiers rather than any contemporary store. Her ensemble had the comfortable assurance of unfashionable mothballed *chic* which struck chords in middle-aged minds and reminded Pennery of pre-war graduation ceremonies for those who'd had time to enjoy their leisurely world in a ten-horse-power motor car from Messrs Rolls & Royce or, goggled with 'cor-blimey' cap peak reversed, crouched low over handle-bars of a noisy *'Built absolutely without regard to cost'* Pioneer Motorcycle.

Young Miss Parroty bicycled everywhere on a stately machine which, like its owner, reminded onlookers of a bygone age, referring to it as "My faithful Iron Horse" and embarrassing whoever could not avoid her by confiding, "I call her Dorcas because, as you will know from your Bible, Dorcas was famous for *her good deeds and gifts of mercy.*"

It had a high frame, large wheels with fatly-tubular tyres which had to be specially ordered; threading its rear mudguards chastely tinted silk cords prevented a full skirt catching in the spokes. Strapped to the handlebars was a capacious wicker-basket to the front of which was secured a beautifully polished wide-lensed cycle-lamp which had never ever been used; perhaps just as well for, as it was acetylene-powered like the cine-projector, had she attempted to light it, at the very least she would have singed her eyebrows. As a girl she had been told by her father never to cycle home in the dark because she might attract 'unwelcome attentions', although nobody in Salter's Creek had ever been even kissed in the dark unless they wanted to be kissed, it did not disperse his pessimistic mistrust of the human race. He had died at a ripe old age satisfied that her honour had been saved time and again by his timely advice, blissfully unaware that his daughter's literal interpretation of his stricture had never prevented her *walking* home in the dark *pushing* the bicycle, convinced that lighting the lamp was an invitation to rapists.

On the evening of 'Mayor' Loxton's party, the basket was, as usual on a Tuesday, stuffed with music. Parking 'Dorcas' carefully at one side of the porch, she fished in her capacious handbag for the key. Young Miss Parroty was particularly proud of the key. For many years she had trotted round to Patterson each Tuesday and Friday to collect the key until one day Patterson had suggested she should have a key of her own; a unique privilege. From that moment Patterson could do no wrong; she, of all the women in Slater's Creek, had 'Been Chosen' to have a 'Special Place' in the spiritual life of the community.

Until then she had always felt subordinate to her elder sister but now she acquired a new self-confidence. She began to appear on committees, first just as an ordinary member but soon as Secretary until it had reached the stage that whenever somebody was needed to act as Secretary, Young Miss Parroty came to mind. A byword for discreet efficiency, she was currently Secretary to seven committees which met monthly and three others which met only two or three times a year. Young Miss Parroty had discovered that her *niche* was to be indispensable and she relished it. The committees depended on her, the church music depended on her and, above all, Leonard Patterson depended on her.

Humming *O God our help in Ages past,* she entered the church. It was darker than expected. She reached the organ loft with some difficulty as temporary access was in the form of a ladder; Loxton had proved less tractable than usual in the matter of making repair funds available. Patterson had told her in confidence, that they would not get matters settled satisfactorily until Loxton's damaged ankle had ceased to give unexplained twinges. She switched on only the light over the organ keyboard; as Secretary-Treasurer to the Church Fabric and Finance Committee, she was always ostentatiously frugal over the matter of electricity in order to set an example. She could not resist lingering a moment and tried a few bars of *The Trumpet Voluntary* on the organ. Another improvisation on that? She wondered if it would be suitable but had to admit to herself that switching convincingly from the Collection hymn tune to improvisation without pause demanded a finesse which was frequently lacking. The organ hummed electrically and, in lieu of any other sound, its soft noise filled the church.

She turned to go down again; there was still her enormous handbag and the rest of the music to be fetched. Light from the organ loft partially illuminated the aisle; daylight almost departed, there was otherwise only the fading glow from the great window with its tinted panes high behind the altar. Although the far end of the church was muted and indistinct she thought there was somebody there. Taking off her spectacles with the innate reverence a man takes off his hat in church. "Good evening…Vicar?" she questioned loudly, tentatively in her 'praying' voice. She was the only person in the entire town who called their minister 'Vicar'.

She came carefully down the final step and moved reverently along the aisle, the praying figure, virtually prostrated at the altar-rail too absorbed to acknowledge her. *A woman in a black dress…?* How foolish of her! *It's his cassock of course!* Not wishing further to disturb her beloved Mr Patterson, she turned to go, as she did so her eye caught something shining blackly on the polished wooden floor beside him.

The praying figure was very still. *Uncannily still?* Young Miss Parroty had never known Patterson pray at night and he had never prostrated himself – at least she had never known him to do so. *Was it something he did only when he thought there was nobody else about?* She squinted at the gleaming thing on the floor beside him. Not a thing but a *stain? Someone has spilled a bottle of Indian ink on our church floor!* As Secretary to the Church Fabrics Committee Young Miss Parroty authoritatively replaced her spectacles before indignantly stepping closer.

Not ink.

Blood.

ii

Loxton's birthday party was going well as it always did but now, with reports of The Great Blaze moving relentlessly east before an increasingly less gentle breeze, the evening provided a moment to relax. There were drinks, not in improper profusion, but certainly in plenty. The room was packed, the Loxtons at their hospitable best. Somewhere a rather grand new gramophone was playing music from *Show Boat* – still attracting packed houses in New York – which nobody in Salter's Creek had seen but of which everyone had heard. Windows open, voices spilled out across the close-cropped grass and flowers which graced the garden of which Loxton was so proud. Beyond, across a narrow sidewalk, waited a line of dusty pony-traps and an occasional car; although many of those present had walked, a greater number than usual had come in from outlying homesteads.

Salter's Creek had no truck with the dainty cocktail-party sophistication of city living. It liked its food either good and solid, or highly decorative and sweet, preferably both: a superb array of snacks cakes and sandwiches surrounded a magnificent iced cake. Numerous smaller satellite tables carried the overflow. If the layout echoed Kip's abandoned birthday celebration that was only because this was the way all parties *should* look according to Salter's Creek.

The party was being held in the house Henry and Bella Loxton had inherited shortly after they were married. Childless themselves, they eventually dispensed with the walls between what had been his childhood nursery, his nanny's former bedroom and the main ground-floor room, turning it into 'The Mayor's Parlour' where virtually all their social and much of the official, entertaining took place. The ugly, wind-weathered-grey Municipal Building, a rambling pile next to the police station off McCutcheon Square, was used only when central government civil servants made one of their blessedly-rare visitations.

Affectionately referred to as 'Mayor' for nearly forty years by all, including those who had been at school with him and were well aware it was mishearing of his first name, it was agreed that nobody else could have coped half as well with the numerous tedious administrative chores inflicted by a bureaucracy hundreds of miles away, nor would they have wished to try. Loxton was a popular man; even had there been elections he would never have been opposed.

He called the party to order by energetically ringing a hand-bell. "This isn't a speech," he began, to loud cheers and, with the cheers turning to laughter, he continued, "It's not a complaint either!" A voice shouted "Hear! Hear!" followed by more laughter. "I'd just like to say...great to see you here tonight.... . Thank you all for coming...I didn't know there were so many people in Salter's Creek – perhaps I'll have to look through the Rates list again." (Light-hearted hissing.)

"Finally, let me say, *I'm* at home and..."

"*...AND WE WISH YOU WERE!*" came the chorus.

Cheers, laughter and applause drowned him out: Loxton had said it at his first party, intending of course to imply that everyone should 'make themselves at home' without realising the ambiguity of the actual phrasing he'd used until his wife had pointed it out after the function was over. Since then partygoers had made repeating it part of the tradition.

Somebody began to sing, "*For he's a Jolly good fellow.*" Pennery winced and looked out of a window. He never heard it now without the hair on his neck prickling. It reminded him of slightly un-sober undergraduate contemporaries amongst whom he had numbered three particular friends all of whom had died in mud and squalor on the Western Front. However, with an effort he turned and smiled over at Loxton who beamed back.

And so say all of us-s-s-s
And so say all of us-s-s-s-ss
FORR-O-ORR *HE'S* A JOLLY GOOD FE–ELL...
The door whanged open.
The song died.
Young Miss Parroty stood on the threshold, face alarming

blue-white, ridiculous little hat over one eye, clutching crumpled sheets of music to her breast, stocking ripped and, most unthinkable of all, she wore no glove on one hand.

They could see her throat working, but no words until, like a cork from a bottle, "The-Reverend-Patterson-MA-BD-Dip-Theology-has-been-murdered." Then, very slowly, very distinctly, as though announcing a pianoforte solo at a school concert, or reading the banns, "Tonight. In The Church. At Eight-Thirty." Concluding bizarrely in Coroner's idiom, "By-person-or-persons-unknown."

"But *I* am *here.*" Patterson stepped forward.

Her mouth stayed open, shaking her head, staring as if tranced, whispering, "No! No! No! *NO!* You're *dead* in the *Church!*" before beginning to scream.

The sound tore through the group in the room, out across the garden and road. It was so fierce that everyone seemed paralysed. She stood screaming, on and on, without any apparent in-drawing of breath until Doctor Svensson slapped her face hard. Once! Twice! Each sounding like a pistol report before she collapsed as though suddenly boneless. He caught her as she fell.

"I'll go at once," Randall said quietly to himself, but in the appalled hush everyone heard him.

"I think I should go too." Leonard Patterson stepped forward: "After all, I…ah…appear to be the victim."

He had not the least intention of being funny, but his intervention had the effect of transforming tragedy into farce. A nervous initial high-pitched giggle somewhere at the back infected the room; wave after wave of laughter spread amongst the partygoers. Hopeless, helpless, laughter releasing not only the pent-up tension that had mounted, from the time of Young Miss Parrotys entrance, but also that which had built up in the community over the previous weeks of mysterious fires and the impending threat of The Great Blaze. It was as if hysteria affected them all, glasses and bottles clashed and clinked into a crescendo.

When, that autumn day in 1777, dispirited and helpless in the face of impassable forest tracks, native Indian harassment, useless maps and inefficient support from England, General Burgoyne spent his final hours at Saratoga drinking champagne with his mistress sitting on his knee, before finally surrendering to General Gates, he probably experienced something like the sense of relief that swept through the partygoers in the minutes after Patterson had inadvertently triggered it.

Loxton and Pennery hurried out; laughter and garrulous chatter echoing into the night as though seeking to disinfect every chink and corner where the sound of Young Miss Parroty's screams and the nightly whine of the fire sirens might have lodged. The brittle gaiety of the party seemed to follow Pennery, whirring through the scattered pines behind him like a summer gale as he ran through Loxton's gate to catch the others. They exchanged no word. Hurrying through the darkness, the four of them recognised the relief they had all had experienced was momentary: Patterson was certainly not dead, he was there, walking with them, but something terrible had taken place to put Young Miss Parroty in that state. Uppermost in each of their minds was the realisation that she had merely mistaken the identity of the victim: who would they find lying there in the darkened church?

They came across 'Dorcas'. In her panic, riding in the dark for the first time ever and of course without illumination, her front wheel had struck the side of the road and thrown her off, tearing her stocking. Basket broken and the great lens on the acetylene lamp shattered beyond any repair, it seemed an ominous warning. As of one mind they stopped, took their time trying to straighten the handlebars before carefully putting it upright against a garden wall, trying to convince themselves that restoring bent handlebars was a matter of utmost urgency; anything to delay discovering whatever nameless horror awaited them inside.

Eventually, reluctantly, they forced themselves to go on side by side, no one anxious to lead the way, halting simultaneously at the porch. The wooden door swung open into an uninvitingly black interior. Then, each aware of his own fear as to who they would find, they edged hesitantly forward in unspeaking unison.

Loxton had snatched up his fire-fighter's torch as he left home; its beam preceded them, like a single eye until even that illumination seemed snuffed by distance and darkness. Pennery picked up Young Miss Parrotys gaping handbag. He shuffled forward. Patterson caught his arm.

"No," he said, sharply, "*I* know where the switches are." Secretly the others were relieved it did not have to be them to enter first. He went cautiously into the pitch blackness; the only sounds their heavy breathing and the organ. Even in her panic, Miss Parroty had instinctively switched off the organ-loft light but not the organ itself which continued its eerie moan as if in pain. Their eyes, although becoming accustomed to the gloom, could only make out the less dark arch of the great window. Patterson fiddled in a little wooden cupboard to the right of the door. Each click of a switch sounding almost irreverently intrusive, the lights startled them, springing into action group by group down the aisle, *like squads of disciplined recruits,* Pennery thought to himself.

"Organ loft?" Loxton breathed hard, anxious to turn off the wheezing moan, but looking hesitantly at the ladder.

"I think not," said Patterson as, with another click the organ died with a final sigh, "The altar, I think."

Shoes signalling each hesitant step on the uncarpeted wood, they walked slowly behind him. The aisle seemed as long as the earth itself, the silence, now the organ had ceased, menacing.

Pennery shivered, for an instant back in another place another time – *That ominous silence which seemed to last forever, yet in truth was only minutes, even seconds…waiting for whistles to blow for the despairing scramble up and over the parapet into No Man's Land before…*

"Blood, look there." Randall pointed to the congealed mess shiny black in the yellow light.

"Looks like a woman," Pennery said and stopped. His legs seemed to be seizing up. The other had stopped too, standing abreast, frozen as if they believed that the thing at the altar rail might not really be there unless they went up to it.

"No," whispered Patterson thickly," It's a man, in my cassock."

"Too small for a man," Loxton muttered. Then, with indrawn breath, "Patterson…it's a child!"

Kip! Pennery squeezed his eyes tight, appalled, *I thought he was in bed…*

"Somebody's murdered a *child* in *my* church?" Patterson staggered up to the altar rail and looked down. The whole world seemed to hold its breath.

"Who has done this *infamous thing!*" Patterson's cry rang through the empty building. "This *ungodly, blasphemous* thing!" The Minister turned round and looked back on them. Accusatory, utterly devoid of pity, neither fear nor compassion in his face, only terrible anger.

His tone shocked Pennery. Could the Minister really believe that the murder of a child…Kip…was somehow less obscene than the fact that it had taken place here in his church? As if hypnotised, Pennery forced himself forward.

Sprawled across the altar-rail, draped in one of Patterson's cassocks, head almost severed from the body, paws tied together in hideous mockery of praying hands, lay Pope Potter's huge black dog.

III

AUGUST

…the readiness is all.
Hamlet (5.2.).

13

i

Randall had a hunch. As a good policeman he knew quite well that hunches were treacherous but it nagged away at him; try as he might, he could not put it out of his mind. Restlessly he lay in bed thinking over the events of the evening.

From the moment of their discovery he had, quite illogically, begun to suspect a connection between the fires and desecration of the church. The possibility that these events were connected seemed to have seeped unbidden into his mind preventing him from reviewing the matter rationally or objectively. The sinister connection he inferred for which, he admitted to himself, there was no hard evidence he could put his finger on, distorted his thinking. In a half-doze, first light of dawn peeping through the open window, he re-lived the later events of the previous evening.

The four of them had returned from the church to find the partygoers sobered and anxiously awaiting the truth behind Young Miss Parrotys hysterical revelation. Unsure whether to react with disapproving shock, or regretful levity when they heard about the dog, they settled back into to a more restrained but nonetheless pleasurable night; it would not be until prompted by an editorial in the next edition of *The Sentinel* that an accepted 'party line' would emerge.

Randall had found himself in a corner talking to Pennery, drinking ice-cold beer. Patterson had not stayed.

"I suppose the police don't often have a dog-murder on their hands, Dill?" Pennery was gently ironic. "Who are your suspects? I mean are you going to blame this on my boys too?"

"*I* didn't blame the boys, Pennery, I was only reviewing possibilities." He shook his head and added wryly, "I suppose you could be excused for thinking I've had a bee in my bonnet about the kids ever since that smoking business. It'll be just as well when the summer comes to an end."

"What suspects have you in this case?"

"None. Absolutely no ideas at all. But," he hesitated a little, "just between you and me at the moment, the strange thing is, that I've got firmly fixed in my head the notion that these events are connected."

"The fires you mean? With this dog business? Whatever makes you think that?"

"You've put your finger right on the button, Pennery. That's the trouble, I don't know *why* I think it; it's just a feeling, a hunch if you like. There's something lodged inside my slightly addled brain that's turned a switch and I can't see what. So you're entitled to think my suspicions are quite illogical."

It was strange, Randall thought to himself lying there in the growing light, how fully conversations and thoughts of the day past come back to you when you were dozing off. Scenes too – he could see Pennery putting down his glass and replying: "I agree with you there. To me it does seem illogical to connect this dog business and the fires. Now if it had been something else. Something in the same category, say a bonfire of green wood in the aisle, an attempt to burn down Patterson's church you might have some justification to suspect a connection."

As he lay ruminating on Pennery's remark, Randall was suddenly awake, wide awake. Reminded of his own thoughts when he had been down at the school the day after the four fires something clicked into place. Now he knew he was on the track of his hunch. He screwed his eyes tight as an aid to concentration on their conversation that evening. Pennery had left him at that point to fetch drinks for them both. *What was it I asked Pennery when he returned...?* Something about the boy... That was it! "That boy of yours, is he wild?" *That* was what he'd said to Pennery.

"Of mine? Oh you mean young Kip. No he's not in the *least* wild. In fact the more I see of him the more surprised I am that I ever suspected he might have had any connection at all with the Smokers Club. I think I mentioned before that I believed him then when he said he'd never smoked, well now I'm even more certain that he was telling the truth. He said he'd no idea they were intending to smoke and I'm positive he didn't, not least because his aunt, old Miss Harrison had hatred of cigarettes and a nose as sensitive as a cat's." Pennery paused: "I'm quite sure his presence on that single occasion was entirely accidental, he thought they were going for a swim." Suddenly very serious and positive, "Do you know, Dill, I must confess that I have never ever come across a kid who is so patently, indeed almost painfully, honest." He shook his head. "I find myself increasingly irritated every time I'm told by Patterson that the boy *deliberately* hooked it from church that morning. In no way it was an intentional slight aimed at Patterson, just a nice morning and perhaps he preferred to be outside. Can't say I blame him because Patterson's sermon that day consisted of particularly tendentious moralising."

Their conversation now remained clear and distinct in Randall's memory and a second memory nudged its way forward. When Pennery suggested that perhaps Pope Potter had set the fire alight and he, Randall, had pointed out that Pope Potter had never done such a thing although he'd been around for years, that was when he'd wondered whether a newcomer might be responsible and when he'd remembered Kip was a newcomer. Before the boy's arrival there had been accidental fires, careless fires, but never fires which had been deliberately started. Of course if, despite Pennery's assurance to the contrary, the boy had deliberately absented himself from church because he had a grudge against Patterson…. But why on earth should the lad have taken such a violent a dislike to Patterson in the first place? He shook himself to full wakefulness A little more of their conversation surfaced, he remembered asking idly whether Patterson had complained officially about Kip's absence.

"Yes indeed," Pennery had laughed," I got a note, a formal letter in fact. He suggested, if I remember rightly, something to the effect that a good hiding might do the boy no harm because, and here I quote our revered Minister, "if this sort of ungodliness goes unpunished, who can foretell what might he not get up to in the future?"

"And Kip saw the note?"

"Yes, I thought that when he realised how angry Patterson was, he'd not want to miss again. As I've said already I'm quite sure Kip never intended to annoy anyone. He was really upset by Patterson's suggestion that I shouldn't spare the rod, until I assured him I had no intention of beating him – or indeed anyone else." Pennery had taken a long swallow of beer: "Patterson's been brought up on the Old Testament and Bunyan I shouldn't wonder." An allusion lost on Randall who had never heard of Bunyan.

But Randall, beginning to doze off again, thought to himself, *I suppose that note might well give a kid a real grudge if he thought Patterson was gunning for him.* Something else drifted into his consciousness. The fires had begun only since the boy's arrival in Salter's Creek.... . The boy seemed to have had some sort of quarrel with Patterson, absenting himself from church, inciting the Minister to demand he be punished and taken revenge by desecrating the church.... If that was the situation why not by setting fire to it. *Why the dog?* Once again wide-awake, there came a moment of clarity that Sunday the boy cut church? Had the kid by chance come across Pope Potter preaching, cheeked him and.... *Of course! Pope Potter would have set the dog on him...*Patterson's church and Pope Potter's dog, two birds with one stone!

After the initial excitement of resolving his own particular quandary, Randall closed his eyes again but even as he did so he had already begun to moderate his theories which were, as he had to admit, not even supported by convincing *circumstantial* evidence, but based on mere association of ideas; it did however at least justify further investigation.

He dropped at last into such deep dreamless sleep that he was unaware of a door banging somewhere downstairs. A dawn wind had sprung up and, when he woke the question about Kip Harrison and Pope Potter's dog fell into insignificance.

ii

The wind had grown much stronger. It fanned The Great Blaze, pushing the flames east, carrying still-smouldering embers turning dry trees and even drier undergrowth into a roaring inferno. Twenty miles ahead of it, soldiers were attempting to create a firebreak; every so often an extra-strong gust brought the sound of distant explosions as they dynamited gaps in the thick afforestation.

Homesteaders were already fleeing east, abandoning homes and crops, trying to herd animals before them. A despairing last-minute telephone call from part-time Constable Oates, father of one such family which had waited until the very last minute before surrendering their hard-won living to the devouring flames, apprised Randall of the current situation: over the telephone he could hear the muffled roar of the conflagration like applause in some gigantic stadium.

Fleeing east at the last moment, the road west having become impassable, abandoning homes and crops to the flames, the first refugees appeared mid-morning. Randall urged them to continue further east while they could. From past experience he knew that the influx would worsen and Salter's Creek could hardly accommodate and feed them all. Deterred by Randall's persuasion and the town's obviously limited resources, most moved on. Only those who had friends or relations chose to stay; a few others totally exhausted by vainly attempting to save their homes, took over the remaining just-about-habitable houses around McCutcheon Square which had been abandoned for almost half a century.

The newcomers were a disturbing influence. Until that moment, the township had not envisaged the full terror of the fire. Now, these men and women, dirty, haggard faces, trailing desperately filthy, frightened small children, their older brothers and sisters even more deeply fatigued and shocked than their parents, drew the eyes of everyone in Slater's Creek. *Was this what it was like to fight for and to lose all?*

Pennery's school-term-vacation scheme began to break down. Some children fled further east with their parents, others stayed with relatives in the comparative safety of the township, or temporarily camped down at night in the Small Schoolroom waiting to be collected when their parents finally had to abandon attempting to save their homesteads.

Although those who lived permanently in Salter's Creek itself did not panic, confident that their rocky virtually treeless eminence could not be burnt out in such a comprehensive way, they nevertheless felt menaced as never before. The wind showed no sign of dropping, depositing glowing cinders on window-sills, car roofs, smutting the clothes of those working outside and washing left out to dry.

iii

Presumably unaware that the Biblical name her Gaelic-speaking parents had chosen for their daughter was that of the adulterous wife of the prophet Hosea, Gomer McKay, wife of the man who had fulminated about the Pennery's refusal to thrash all those involved with the Smokers Club, was frequently to be found behind the counter at Parrotys store. The elder Miss Parroty, in her housekeeping *rôle*, also employed her in a domestic capacity at the schoolhouse. One of her tasks was to collect washing, take it to Mr Soong and return the freshly laundered items a couple of days later. She did the same for the Pattersons and, since Joyce had been unwell, had also helped out with other daily chores.

"I thought *somebody* ought to know, Mr Patterson," she whispered with insincere hesitation a couple of days after Loxton's party.

Patterson turned from his desk, "Ah, yes Mrs McKay? Know what?"

"About the dog…"

"The dog…?"

"In the church…" She blushed slightly.

He was immediately alert: "Please do go on!"

"Well not exactly so much about the *dog* as…" Patterson breathed out dismissively which caused her to falter. "Well, the thing is, Mr Patterson, that dog had its throat cut, didn't it?"

Reigning in his impatience, Patterson encouraged her, "Yes you are quite correct."

"Well if someone had done it…done it and didn't want to be found out…what would he do?" Patterson looked blank. "Wouldn't *you* get rid of the knife?" she concluded.

"You've found the knife!" Patterson stood up. "Where is it, we must…?"

"No, no I haven't *found* it."

Penney finally lost patience, "Well then I don't see…"

"But I know of someone who *had* a knife sharp enough and *now* says he's lost it."

"Who?"

"Mr Pennery's boy."

"Kip Harrison ? You say he's lost his knife? The sheath-knife which Eleanor Parroty gave him on his birthday?"

"That's the one. Young Miss Parroty always asks Mr Pennery if Kip's using it and Mr Pennery always says yes *as far as he knows.*" She paused significantly, "But the boy doesn't have it any more… . Yesterday, the morning after Mayor Loxton's 'do' when you found the dog…"

"Yes, yes, go on."

"Well, when I was collecting the laundry from the boy's room to take to Mr Soong…I found the sheath…hidden under his socks… . And it was *empty*. You see what I mean?" she whispered confidentially.

Patterson nodded, but in a way which clearly distanced himself from any hint of intimacy. "You think he's hidden it? Or thrown it away because he killed the dog with it?" *Didn't want it to be found with blood on it of course.*

"Oh, I wouldn't like to say …" in a tone that meant she would very much like to do so "…Though of course it *could* be that! After all he did deliberately stay away from your church and ought to have been punished for it. Just like he should have been with the others in the Smokers Club."

"Mr Pennery is sure he was not one of the smokers!" Patterson said as evenly as he could manage and in a further effort to seem to be objective because Mrs McKay had the reputation of being a notorious gossip, "Young Harrison doesn't seem like the sort of boy who would kill a dog…"

"This morning Young Miss Parroty told me that when she'd asked him he said he used it all the time …" She moved closer, *"You've* never had a family, have you Mr Patterson? You can never tell with *boys* of *that* age, 'specially when they're so… well as if butter wouldn't melt…!" She bustled off leaving the implication hanging in the air.

After she had gone Patterson spent a little time in thought. His mind strayed back to the shoe-lace episode, still irritated by the amused remarks at his expense about his ten suspects. It would wipe off a few smiles and redeem his reputation if he could unmasked the dog-killer. The upshot was that he phoned Pennery insisting that, although quite aware that the school timetable was no longer operating due to the upheaval caused by The Great Blaze, he should send Kip to collect the list of those due to attend Confirmation classes.

Kip arrived, was handed the sheet of paper which Patterson had placed in a large envelope, and was about to run off.

"Have you lost your knife, Kip?" His tone was mild.

"I…I…must have done." Faced with a direct question, Kip was unable to tell an untruth. *Had Patterson found it?*

"Did you still have it yesterday?"

Kip hesitated. "Not really…" he began. *Should he say that it was not until yesterday he'd remembered about the tree…*

"Miss Parroty thinks you still have it." Kip was silent. *How did she know? He hadn't seen her to tell her since he'd lost it.* "So you see I know more than you think." Then sharply, "Now! *When* did you lose it? Or did you *hide* it?"

"Why…well…I didn't *hide* it at all, Mr Patterson, I didn't mean to lose it. It just…got lost."

"Very convenient." *Convenient?* Kip was puzzled. "It seems very strange it should have been only after Mr Loxton's party that it was 'lost'."

"I think it dropped out while I was coming back from a swim."

"It would be far better to tell the truth *now!*" Patterson looked grimmer.

"It *is* the truth, really *it is* the *truth*. I went down to Splash-Puddle for a swim and when I got back I found I'd lost it."

There was a ring of truth which Patterson could not dismiss so easily, but Kip was beginning to feel panic-stricken. *Was his explanation being doubted?* It was a situation he had never met before and he could not understand the fuss about the knife. Unless… Yes! It must be that Young Miss Parroty had complained because he'd not made sure he'd told her enough times that he was enjoying her present, said again how very useful it was. *That must be it.* He wished she had not given him a present.

"Can you remember which day?" Patterson asked meaningfully. "If you are telling the truth, you must remember when it was. After all it was such a fine knife. Did you tell your guardian you'd lost it?" Silence. His lip tightened. "Didn't you mention it to Mr Pennery?"

"I didn't tell anyone about the knife at the time because I thought I knew where it must be. I went back to find it lots of times, an' once…Yes that's right, one time I met 'Mayor' Loxton and helped him carry some moss, I 'spec' he'll remember that."

"Was that the day you lost it?" The reference to Loxton had done much to restore the boy in Patterson's eyes.

"No. No, I'd lost it another day, when I was there at Splash-Puddle with Pope Potter." From Patterson's face he saw he was not nominating a very acceptable witness. "He might remember. I mean he *will* remember because he poured water over me, an' prayed, an' sort of…"

"*Prayed* ? Poured water?" *Was he having his leg pulled?* "And of course you told Mr Pennery all this?"

"Yes, yes, an' that's I when remembered I must'uv left it stuck in the tree."

Patterson frowned, the tale had taken a turn that strained credulity. "So you *pretended* you still had the knife when all the time you'd left it stuck in a tree and now you say it's not there anymore? And you say you told Mr Pennery that you'd lost the knife." His voice ringing with disbelief, "And that Pope Potter poured water over you?"

"Yes. *No*. I di'n't *pretend* I had it the *first* the time when I told Mr Pennery about Pope Potter, I di'n't tell him then 'cos I was sure I'd dropped it on the way home so it wasn't really *lost* because I thought I knew where it would be when I went back to find it the next day…but I couldn't find it though I looked fer days…an'… an' I…" becoming almost incoherent, "I only jus' remembered… Las' night that is… that I'd stuck it in the tree…an' it's not there now an' I've been back today an' I'd've seen it… *Really* Mr Patterson it's *gone* an' *now* it really *is* lost an' I—" on the verge of tears. "What's the matter? What'm'I s'posed to've done?"

"You 'stuck it *in a tree*'!" Kip was about to explain that it was as a hat-peg for the boater but Patterson, voice laced with sarcasm, ploughed on, "You say that you've been back and the knife in the tree had gone!" Total disbelief. "Kip, just tell me the truth. *You* killed Pope Potter's dog in my church last night didn't you?"

"*Me* ! You mean *me*?" The horror in his voice was high. "Kill his dog?" Tears tipped down his cheeks. Patterson was almost convinced of the boy's innocence after all He felt a fleeting moment of compassion. *Had he perhaps gone too far?*

"Come, come Kip. I had to ask. I really had to ask. No need to cry!" Patterson put an arm on his shoulder. "It's all right, I'm sure Mr Pennery will remember you telling him. Have you any idea who might have done it?"

"No! *Nnnno!*" Wrenching himself free Kip fled out into the sun, frightened by Patterson's accusation but, above all, bitterly ashamed of his tears.

Pre-occupied with his conviction that he had found the culprit responsible for both the mysterious fires and the desecration of his church he had forgotten his wife's delicate situation and that she was sleeping upstairs. Awoken by voices Joyce Patterson had come to the top of the stairs just in time to hear "No! Nnnno!" as the boy tore himself away from her husband's apparently embracing arm.

His hand still reaching to comfort the boy as he fled, Patterson turned and saw her standing there. "You know, Joyce, I don't think Pennery really is right for that boy. It seems to me he's unfit as guardian." She was standing still looking at him. Or was it through him? "Are you all right, dear?"

"All right. Of course *I'm* all right." Her voice was high. "How *can* you go on like this, Leonard? Think of me!"

It was a cry of anguish. The full realisation of her agony came back to him. How foolish of him to assume she had overcome her disappointment of their failed bid to look after Kip. He admonished himself inwardly for not waiting to talk to the boy until she was out of the house. He really must contact the adoption people as soon as she was more…settled. "I do think of you, Joyce dear. I'm so sorry that I…" His sympathetic tone melted her hysteria a little.

"Oh, *Leonard*…"

Anxious to break the silence which seemed somehow accusatory, he turned the conversation to a quite different topic "Is it your sermon, dear? Is there a problem with it? My turn to ask *you* this time, isn't it?" he smiled.

She did not smile back. "There is no problem, Leonard!"

Joyce Patterson had happy memories of her earliest childhood in the halcyon days before her father's disgrace. Each August the parish had honoured Margaret Clitherow, Roman Catholic martyr who, together with her unborn child, had been pressed to death under seven or eight hundredweight of stones placed on her by her Protestant neighbours at the toll-booth on Ouse Bridge in August 1586. It had become customary each year for an address from the pulpit to be given by a woman. Her mother had been one of the regular speakers and had formed an inter-denominational group calling for canonisation and a Feast Day at the end of August with whom Joyce still corresponded in her mother's memory. After their marriage Joyce had persuaded her husband to conduct a similar service on the last Sunday in August when she would give an address commemorating the martyrdom. "I think I now have the ideas for it."

She spoke so oddly that he looked at her more closely; she really was not any better. "Sure it won't be too much for you?"

"No Leonard. No, I must do it. especially now." Then, very distinctly, "There are important things I need to say."

Later, at tea she asked casually why Kip Harrison had been there, listening tight-lipped with disbelief when he told her he suspected Kip might have desecrated the church.

iv

Patterson did not like loose ends. The following day he taxed Pennery with the significance of the lost knife.

"You're blaming *Kip* for *killing the dog!*"

"Ah well… I'm just saying we must be *sure*, mustn't we? After all, first his parents, then his great aunt and now…he might be well…*disturbed*…getting a bit *wild* perhaps?" Implying the schoolmaster's lax discipline was to blame, but Pennery was too incredulous to notice the implication. "Did he tell you *when* he lost it? Or *where?"*

"Yes. One afternoon when he went to bathe at Splash-Puddle. He also told me Pope Potter threw water at him! And he says that he'd told you that."

"That's right! Pope Potter…Of course the old boy's dotty."

"What I want to know," Patterson persisted, "is *when* did it happen. The boy was vague."

Pennery briefly prevaricated with himself, recognising the conclusions the Minister might chooses to draw from what he was about to say. "The day before the night of the fire," Patterson impatiently shifted from foot to foot, "I can be quite definite because that was the evening Kip was rather late for supper."

"Which fire? We're always having fires."

"That first fire at Splash-Puddle. The one right at the beginning," adding, in case Patterson doubted his memory, "I was woken by the departure of the fire squad."

It was not until some minutes after they had parted that the full implication struck Patterson. "Kip was home rather late…" *from Splash-Puddle…* . Open-mouthed, he stood stock-still in McCutcheon Square. Kip Harrison had been at Splash-Puddle the very afternoon the first holly fire was being prepared…*but when I questioned them all about the broken shoelace, Kip Harrison never admitted he'd been at Splash-Puddle…*ignoring the fact that, in his anxiety to identify the owner of the broken lace, he had entirely omitted to ask when any of them had last bathed at Splash-Puddle.

Pope Potter was an obvious blind. Did that boy really believe that anyone would consider the old man capable of providing a coherent, let alone reliable witness statement? As for all that nonsense about having water poured over him! Sheer fantasy! *The boy had taken him in completely.* Tears? *Probably turns them on and off like a tap.* The boy had obviously been there gathering holly, building the fire and, thanks to the schoolmaster's lack of supervision, sneaking out to set it alight the following night. If Patterson was triumphant, he was also disappointed with himself. He had been far too sympathetic, far too soft with the boy; had he been firmer, more forceful, the boy would have confessed.

One other point which needed clearing up; Kip claimed Loxton had seen him returning from his knife hunt one evening. He telephoned Loxton who confirmed that Kip had carried the sack of moss all the way back, he was just as certain there had been no reference whatever to having been searching for his 'lost' knife. *Surely the boy would have mentioned had he really lost such a cherished birthday present?* Though Loxton could not remember the precise date, it was certainly some days after the Splash-Puddle fire. As Loxton put down the phone he could not help wondering why the Minister thought the date so important.

His call ended, Patterson sorted out in his mind the order of events as they now seemed to have occurred. Although Kip had told Pennery about the lost knife, he had not done so until much later than the evening on which he had first related seeing Pope Potter at Splash-Puddle – if indeed such a meeting had ever occurred other than in the boy's imagination. No, the first Pennery had heard of the lost knife was just before he had set out for Loxton's party, an hour or so before Miss Parrotys grisly discovery in the church.... Furthermore the boy had been at Splash-Puddle when the first fire was being prepared...*in which case I wonder whether…*

Patterson got up and walked purposefully to the church.

As he suspected there was a great deal of dust. The cleaner, daughter of limited intelligence from a badly-off forest family, refused to continue her duties on the grounds that there might be a murderer still lurking. He looked round. Nothing untoward. He was about to leave when he turned back, strode behind the altar and peered beneath it, discovering evidence that brought Randall hurrying to the spot.

There, in the dark shadow, was a small, purposefully heaped cone of green leaves beside which lay a grubby medicine-bottle half full of paraffin. Either the fire had gone out before it took hold, or the firebug had been disturbed in the act of setting a match to it by Young Miss Parrotys arrival for her organ practice. He (they all believed it was 'he') must have hidden there beneath the altar, making-off without lighting it the moment she vanished in hysterics?

Randall did not say much, but listened to Patterson's slightly incoherent conviction that Kip Harrison was the culprit – *Firebug! Dog-killer! Church Desecrator!*

Having himself heard about the missing knife from Loxton for the first time only late that afternoon he began, albeit reluctantly, to admit that Patterson's reasoning seemed to have some validity. The evidence that there had indeed been an attempt to fire the church threw him back to the suspicion which had surfaced dozing in bed after the party, that the desecration of the church and the outbreak of fires were connected. Now the 'lost' knife certainly refocused his attention on the possible guilt of young Harrison. He telephoned Loxton.

When Patterson returned to the Manse, he found a scrawled barely legible note in his wife's hand: there had been a phone call:

Dill wants you to phone him.

"Did he say what it was about?" he asked her as she poured tea.

"Something to do with that Harrison boy." *Why was she lowering her voice?*

He picked up the phone, Randall answered at once. "Thought I'd let you know that I've spoken to Loxton and he remembers Kip helping him with his sack of moss. Though the boy made no mention of any lost knife then." He paused and cleared his throat "Thing is, Henry's certain that it was the evening of those four fires. And it now turns out the boy was at Splash-Puddle the day before that first fire." He sighed. "Building it perhaps?" Another sigh. "I think we'd better meet."

"Of course, I'll be there. When? Oh yes of course…The Great Blaze? Let me know when you.ve decided." Patterson replaced the phone triumphantly, last doubts dissolved, his theory vindicated. Despite the embarrassment over the broken laces it was turning out as he, Patterson, had suspected all along, one of that smoking gang, almost certainly the very boy who had disrespected his Sunday service due to the schoolmaster's laxity. He went to bed elated, unaware that Loxton's cryptic message mentioning both Kip Harrison and the Salter's Creek's policeman, together with the policeman's request for a meeting had been overheard by his wife and interpreted in a very different way.

14

i

I still find it difficult to believe that Kip Harrison had anything to do with the fires or the church business whatever Patterson says." Loxton puffed at an impossible pipe which he smoked only when he could make the effort.

"I think you could be right, Henry. But I'm afraid that Mrs McKay is an unrepentant gossip and she'll tell everyone." His wife sat composedly beside a large table lamp, mending some delicate garment of her own. "I don't think Dill's absolutely convinced either." She threaded a needle. "The boy seems very likeable to me."

"But perhaps Pennery was a mistake. Too easy-going. Too… too *lenient* that's the word."

"Is it too late?"

"For what, Bella dear?"

"Why, to get somebody else to take him in."

"It might upset Pennery." Loxton paused: "Though I'm not

so sure." He paused again. "Come to think of it I doubt whether he minds one way or the other."

"What about it then?"

"The trouble is who? The Pattersons?"

"I suppose so. I mean I could sound out Joyce, I'm going to look in to see how she is tomorrow morning."

"The Randalls would be far too busy." He puffed again." I suppose we might…at a pinch."

"No, not us, Henry. You're too busy and I don't want to be responsible for a child, not now at our age. I wouldn't be good as a stepmother. There must be others, but first I'll try Joyce."

"Do it carefully, after all she hasn't been well and Patterson swears it's because of her having set her heart on the kid in the first place. Furthermore Pennery may not agree. Anyhow, if Patterson's right about the dog and the fires they'll hardly want to take on a delinquent."

"I'm sure he's not a delinquent, but he may be troubled, who wouldn't be after his mother, father and great aunt have all died on him so to speak, but I'm sure he's not a delinquent, Henry. Anyway I'll take care."

The following morning she approached the subject obliquely. "Is your husband fond of the boy?" Bella Loxton asked casually, perhaps too casually for the mere mention Kip's name put Joyce Patterson on her guard.

"No! No he certainly is not! They hate the sight of each other."

Taken aback by the vigour of Joyce Patterson's totally unexpected response, Bella Loxton said carefully, "But I seem to remember you'd offered to take him in the first place so I thought…"

"That was earlier!" Joyce Patterson interrupted. "Since then we've changed our mind." The memory of Kip sneaking from the house that Saturday afternoon weeks before, his tearful departure from her husband's arms only days earlier and the cryptic telephone message the previous evening determined her response. She knew what had been taking place. *Kip, having rejected Leonard's advances, had told Pennery who informed Randall and Loxton.* Now even Bella Loxton, her erstwhile friend were gathering evidence.

However, now that the crisis had come, her plan of action was clear. In her anxiety to dissuade what, in her overwrought state, seemed to be probing, questions, she had decided to imply that Leonard Patterson positively disliked the boy. She would make it clear to them all that the boy was acting against Leonard out of pure spite.

✳

"I gathered from Joyce that Leonard is well... actually *hated* by the boy," Bella reported at lunch. "It seems young Harrison resented getting a ticking-off for something."

"Probably about cutting church that day," Loxton observed that evening, when he related his wife's conversation with Joyce Patterson to Randall. He attached less importance to it than Randall who determined to investigate for himself; Patterson's allegations and Mrs McKay's revelation had already begun to give rise to rumours as to the probable the identity of the firebug.

Thus it was that the following morning, whilst Patterson, stubbornly undeterred by the disruption to the school caused by the advance of The Great Blaze, took a much depleted Confirmation class, Randall went in search of Joyce Patterson. She had lived the scene so often in her mind that, this time, far from seeming hysterical she was ice cool.

No, she could not be absolutely certain what had provoked such vitriolic hatred. Yes, her husband had, quite understandably, recommended corporal punishment for deliberately missing the Sunday service. Had Pennery perhaps done as suggested and punished the boy too severely? (Randall knew that was not the case but, he admitted to himself, Kip had certainly been shown Patterson's letter.)

"That boy is untruthful," and almost without breathing it seemed to Randall, she rushed on, "Leonard is sure he lied about not smoking three years ago. They *all* were! Could *anyone* believe him now, about 'losing' his knife so conveniently, just before the desecration of the church? Might he not have a grudge against Pope Potter too? Perhaps the old man discovered him lighting fires in the forest and walloped him. Or even set that dog on him." Although her husband's brief report of Kip's explanation contained little detail of what had taken place, he had been deliberately unspecific in such a way as to imply that there might be something to account for the death of the dog as a form of retaliation. Finally, slyly, she concluded, "Don't *you* think there something odd about the boy's account of that so-called bathing incident at Splash-Puddle?"

Randall, who had been intending only to ascertain whether or not Kip had encountered Patterson other than for Scripture lessons, found his logical mind reeling under the welter of accusation delivered almost as though rehearsed. Although there was nothing too far-fetched in her accusation, the sheer volume of fact (or was it merely innuendo?) made him uneasy. He thanked Joyce Patterson and left.

Smiling, she watched him from the window, convinced she had established her husband's innocence once and for all, unaware that her passionate defence had left Randall wondering precisely what had been going on between Patterson and the boy that upset his wife so much.

Turning back to her husband's desk, Bible open beside her, she began writing again, her large sprawling hand covering sheet after sheet. Had Leonard Patterson come in he would have been concerned by the beads of perspiration across her forehead, alarmed by tiny points of saliva at the corners of her mouth.

The whereabouts of his knife nagged at Kip, not only before he fell asleep as it had done at first, but all the time. Establishing the fact that he really had left the knife there by the pool was now all-important. He kept an eye out for Pope Potter, certain that the old man could help exonerate him if he chose although, mindful of Pennery's warning, he no longer wanted to meet him alone; but nobody had seen him for days. Stories of the severed head proliferated; *The Sentinel* had printed a gruesome description. What if the old man had found his birthday knife and had killed the dog with it? Why would he kill his own dog unless he'd gone mad? Might the old man kill him too? *Had the old man intended to do exactly that at Splash Puddle?*

After another fruitless search he ran back to the school. Nothing made sense. Patterson's questions did not make sense. The mysterious fires did not make sense. He thought back over the summer. Patterson's letter about him cutting the service seemed to have revived memories of the Smokers Club and because of that he was now suspected of starting the green-wood fires although he'd never been one of them. His birthday feast had vanished under a ribbon of ants. Was it all God's punishment for missing church that Sunday? His stomach tightened: it was as if formerly friendly, welcoming Salter's Creek had been turned inside out. Normally he would have shunned even contemplating invading the emotional distance which he and the schoolmaster had established between them. He remembered how, when he was four or five, he had related the small woes of the day as he sat secure and cherished on his father's knee. At that moment, he would have given anything to know the security of that same comforting intimacy with Pennery: to be able to talk to him about Pope Potter, the dog, the lost knife, the fires, Patterson's accusations. Above all, to be rescued from a chilling fear at the heart of which was the terrifying loneliness that gripped him so suddenly and completely.

Sight of the schoolhouse restored his self-confidence, its homeliness buoyed him up again: the childish yearning to share his fears intimately with Pennery melted away and, although he did not know it, the chance to establish his innocence vanished with it.

ii

Overnight the wind rose again. It carried The Great Blaze forward even more quickly than before. The following afternoon it would reach the firebreak and the army had already begun to draw back. A constant stream of vehicles threaded the road, the shrill whine of overheated cars and whirr of heavy army-truck tyres was borne into the township throughout the night. By morning individual clots of refugee vehicles had coalesced into one slow-moving, virtually unbroken column. Although much of this sad traffic bypassed the slip-road to Salter's Creek, many drew in for petrol; Loxton, anxious to preserve enough fuel should they themselves have to be evacuated, ensured the filling station rationed passing vehicles to no more fuel than would get them to Cranston.

A few of the fleeing settlers who had waited until the last possible moment before abandoning their homes drew in to take what would turn out to be temporary refuge in the treeless safety of Salter's Creek. They had hung on almost too long, watching the maw of flame inexorably swallow up the hard-won farms which grudged them their hard-won living, despairing as it gobbled up careful hardwood plantings and heard tall indigenous pines explode with deafening reports. They had failed to prevent flames taking mouthful after mouthful of the untamed land which they, their fathers and grandfathers had, with sweat, axe and plough, chivvied into small pastures and modestly productive grain-fields, leaving behind nothing but smouldering stumps, blackened stubble, charred carcasses of livestock. However fast they moved, the flames seemed close behind; jealous, avenging Furies pursuing the incomers for their temerity in daring to take such liberties with the wilderness which, since time immemorial, it had been *their* privilege to destroy by fire. In their heart of hearts these dispirited refugees no longer believed that even the military firebreak would or could halt the onslaught.

Two of the Salter's Creek emergency fire squads were called out and departed, sirens wailing, into the night, one half an hour after the other. A third was on stand-by. Some volunteers, those who had decided to stay temporarily in Salter's Creek, thus increasing the manpower available, were veterans of their own vain attempts at first for days, then weeks, to halt The Great Blaze.

Randall, who led the second group, could see their particular conflagration long before they reached it. It was well alight but it was possible to see that here too it had been deliberately started; scraps of oily rag were clearly evident. Although they dowsed it, they returned at dawn with the demeanour of beaten men. Fires caused by nature, or even by accident, they could understand – that was the will of God, or even malign gods – but fires deliberately started in such remote spots demoralised them.

The second group arrived back just as the rising sun behind the huge smoke pall of The Great Blaze reddened its edges until it looked as though fire had engulfed the entire visible world and for many of the weary firefighters it might just as well have done so; their pessimistic disillusionment spread like plague.

Loxton, sooty, damp with exertion, conferring with Randall, agreed that his fire too might well have been intentional. It had burned out its base area, but in such a difficult to access spot, it seemed unlikely it was the accidental carelessness of a casual wanderer. Indeed it was doubtful whether anyone would have been foolish enough to consider camping in view of The Great Blaze to the west.

In the hope of preventing further conflagrations, Randall tried to summon military help from the east by radio. Nobody could be spared: manpower was deemed to be more valuable fighting flames they could see than patrolling currently fire-free zones in the slight hope of thwarting a possible fireraiser. Moreover there was little chance of anything less than a division of soldiers being able to prevent a determined man from setting fires in virtually inaccessible spots if that was his perverted intention.

Not only were these conflagrations very clearly intended to set the forest ablaze but, unlike the earlier smoke-creating green-wood fires, these locations followed no predictable north, south, east, and west compass-point pattern, but had been set here, there, everywhere east of Salter's Creek.

Weary when he had arrived back, Randall felt even more tired when he had finished writing his report. He bathed and staggered into bed. At five o'clock Edith woke him: the third squad had been called away on another job also to the east. Utterly exhausted, too befuddled by sleep to take it in, mumbling instructions to be called only if his physical presence was vital, he slept until noon. Then he went to the office. The Great Blaze had, it seemed, been halted, if only temporarily, by the militarily constructed firebreak.

That night there were three more fires. Most of the remaining men in the township were called out at one time or another, the last squad returned with the dawn. One blaze at least had been deliberate, the others it was impossible to determine. However, they had all been in less inaccessible places; one at least might have been started by glowing embers borne on the wind from The Great Blaze.

During the rest of the day no further rogue fires were reported, but at dusk two thin spirals of smoke were spotted by a sharp-eyed observer in the Three Pines tower and both outbreaks were quelled easily. For the first time for weeks so it seemed, everyone was back before midnight. There had been one casualty; Owens, owner of the saw mill, had tripped and fallen heavily. His leg was broken, but he had been in no danger. Only one outbreak demanded action the following night and that seemed a genuine accident, starting not far from the verge of the main road. Perhaps it was all over?

As soon as he was recovered enough, Randall applied himself again to his reports, then to marking up the maps. With the exception of the last outbreak, all the least accessible fires which they had only just managed to reach before they took hold of the surrounding undergrowth had been east of Salter's Creek. Was the firebug creating another impassable inferno to the east, sandwiching them between it and the Great Blaze? Perhaps it was only a figment of his exhaustion and lack of sleep, but ought he to encourage women and children to leave whilst the road was still passable? Kennethina Biggelow had already gone east to Cranston in her much envied Model 40, 36 horsepower Durant, the handsome marmalade cat which she had adopted (or had adopted her?) as an abandoned feral kitten the evening of her husband's death, sitting imperiously in the passenger seat. However, envisaging the consternation which might ensue if he ordered evacuation, he blamed his overwrought imagination for contemplating such an extreme course of action. The virtually treeless 'island' of Salter's Creek might be uncomfortable, but in the past it had survived innumerable forest fires. Nevertheless the fact remained that he suspected the most recent fires to the east had also been deliberately started. He decided say nothing of his fear to Loxton, nor even to his wife for the time being.

Forty miles west, The Great Blaze reached the firebreak, roaring impotently at the militarily cleared space, which thwarted further progress. Behind it, nothing but blackened stumps; the flames seemed to be dying down at last, sparks no longer jumped high into the air as trees, reduced to an incandescent mass toppled into the inferno. Standing at the far edge of the firebreak, heat still forcing them to squint their eyes, groups of exhausted military firefighters watched anxiously for the final red embers to die into unthreatening blackness.

They were to be disappointed; just before dawn swirling up-currents caused by the enormous heat from the blackened forest floor built for a brief time into mini-tornados, whirling sparks from the still smouldering ground high into the air and a sudden sharp breeze jumped enough of them across the firebreak to set loose the fire in a dozen new places.

By breakfast time it was common knowledge that The Great Blaze, having leaped the final obstacle, was making for Salter's Creek and the heavily forested country beyond. The army contingents fell back and began, vainly, to try to establish another firebreak. Time was short and the unwelcome breeze, although it had lessened again, gently pushed the flames before it. Pennery stood on the knoll below the tower at Three Pines Rough with Randall. In the distance, though not now as great a distance as was any longer comfortable, tall redwood pines glowed momentarily like incandescent globes before bursting into flames with an ear-splitting crack.

Salter's Creek became alive with animals, flocks, herds, singly:

fox, bear, wild dogs, wolves, cats, squirrels, rabbits, mice and dozens of other rodents. They took no notice of either humans or other animals, hardly bothering to avoid even McCutcheon Square at the centre of the township, so single-purposed and headlong was their flight. A huge bear was shot by Rogerson as he brought his wife and children into town, before returning to attempt to rescue what he still could from their threatened home.

Those few refugees who had halted hoping they need flee no further, began quietly to leave, joining the crawling queue of cars and trucks: they had no wish to stay until driven on by flames close behind them for a second time. The population of Salter's Creek was almost back to normal; it eased the food situation, but there were fewer fire-fighters.

That night, at last, the wind dropped away altogether and, miraculously there were no new rogue fires reported. However, the smell of burning hung heavy in the now-still air; it was gloomy even at midday on account of the smoke. The Great Blaze appeared content merely to nibble its way closer, which seemed somehow more menacing.

Those long resident were relying on their slight but rocky eminence that had kept them safe in the past. They had already felled any trees however small which had strayed within the town boundary or been planted in gardens, carting them away to a place in the forest where they would be burnt without harm to anyone should the flames eventually find them. Except for the tower at Three Pines Rough, Salter's Creek looked comfortingly naked of fire hazards and for a while they all tried to pretend that life had returned to normal.

15

The inhabitants of Slater's Creek were sensible people at heart, but the threat of all-consuming fire was too immediate to promote calm or reasoned discussion. Matters were not helped by *The Sentinel* dwelling on the menace of an elusive firebug, the mysterious beheading of the dog, even implying that perhaps the invasion of ants at Kip's party had been some sort of warning that **Forces of Darkness** were massing against them.

Although conscious that, realistically, it was likely to be merely a lull before the final onset of The Great Blaze, now only twenty miles away, Randall knew he must take any opportunity to the get to the truth of the desecration of the church, which was becoming a matter of aggressively ill-informed speculation.

Tired and increasingly concerned about the impending menace of The Great Blaze, Randall could not however dismiss his unease about Kip's Splash-Puddle bathe. That was where they had found the first green-wood fire. What had Pope Potter been doing there? *Why with the boy?* He became even more thoughtful... . The deliberate fires... the desecration of the church, evidence that a fire there had been intended there too and now doubt as to when Kip had lost his knife, if indeed he really had lost it as he claimed. *Could such a young boy really be responsible? For the fires? The dog?* He seemed such a nice kid whenever he'd spoken to him. However, it needed to be resolved before it got altogether out of hand, before accusations based on Patterson's suspicions were voiced publically.

Action had to be taken, leadership offered, before hotheads demanded that their Jonah be rooted out and sacrificed to the Gods regardless of who it seemed to be. Randall was not a fanciful man but he understood what hysteria and fear could do; an experienced policeman, he appreciated the necessity of getting matters settled as soon as possible. If anyone ought to know what the boy had been up to that afternoon at Splash-Puddle, it would be the schoolmaster. Moreover, it was high time to define precisely the obligations of Kip Harrison's guardianship; should the boy remain with Pennery? The source of the mysterious fires and the virtual decapitation of Pope Potter's dog, once resolved, Salter's Creek would face up to the threat posed by The Great Blaze like rational individuals rather than a superstitious mob. He phoned the schoolmaster, asking him to join the meeting provisionally arranged with Patterson and Loxton and Pennery wholeheartedly endorsed the decision to try to resolve matters before the current of fear of immolation undermined the normally equable tenor of communal life.

They gathered in Loxton's office. Young Miss Parroty, as well as being the 'witness' who had given Kip the missing knife was, inevitably, present in her Secretarial *persona* to take notes. Because it was largely at Patterson's insistence that Randall had been persuaded to convene the meeting, the Minister insisted on speaking first. Although Randall, after further reflection, now found himself doubtful of Kip Harrison's involvement, Patterson had no doubt whatsoever that the boy was connected with both the desecration of the church and the fires. Scarcely drawing breath, he spoke rapidly, thrusting his words forward as if afraid they would get away from him before he had completed his damning interpretation of what he referred to as "the indisputable facts of the matter".

"There's not much doubt is there?" Young Miss Parroty, his long-time disciple was immediately convinced; she looked round expectantly.

"Hmmm." Loxton sucked at his pipe which had gone out. "I'm not quite clear..." Then, anxious not to seem to be condemning her, added apologetically, "I fear I must be rather a slow thinker."

"What do you think, Pennery?" prompted Randall.

"Well, on the face of it there would *seem* to be a case," Pennery said, slowly and carefully. "Mind you, I don't believe Kip would do anything like this. He doesn't seem to me to be that sort of boy." He paused: "Nevertheless perhaps we ought to give what Patterson says our full consideration."

Unfortunately Pennery's judicial objectivity led them to infer that although it was his duty to his orphaned ward, at least to question Patterson's allegations, the schoolmaster believed it possible (even *probable?*) that the boy was responsible. It was the sort of guarded response that they themselves might have made regarding somebody in their own family who could not be betrayed in public, but was clearly guilty of a misdemeanour: even Patterson felt that, had he been Kip's guardian, it would have been his duty vigorously to protest the boy's innocence whatever he suspected to the contrary. This misinterpretation of the schoolmaster's apparently unimpassioned reaction to the Minister's accusations began to re-colour even Loxton's thinking.

They were doing Pennery an injustice: his intellectual instinct demanded that the reasons for Patterson's accusations should be examined in detail in order for them to be convincingly refuted because he was quite certain this would establish his ward's innocence once and for all.

Ironically, had Pennery adopted the line of argument they expected of him by strongly refuting Patterson's accusation, passionately defending Kip's innocence, confronting the Minister, demanding Patterson should supply irrefutable proof instead of mere supposition based on the flimsiest circumstantial evidence, it would have created a situation explosive enough to necessitate finding and questioning Pope Potter, which would have revealed the stark truth of the matter.

Breaking the pause after Pennery had spoken, Randall was careful not to encourage them to jump to conclusions. He realised that not only had the inquiry become in all but judicial formality a trial, but that it was no ordinary one. Not only was the defendant himself absent, but he was represented by a man who saw his function not so much as the accused's advocate, but as an utterly objective impartial judge. "Pennery's right. We must look at it closely and ascertain what precisely is fact and what merely supposition. After all it is quite possible that however it looks at the moment, the boy was not involved in any way at all other than having met Pope Potter at Splash-Puddle by chance and genuinely losing the knife that may, I stress *may*, have been used on the dog." Looking across at Patterson, "As far as *I* am aware no knife has yet been found?" Reluctantly the Minister shook his head. "In the church? Behind the altar for instance?" Another shake of the head. "Let's take events in sequence," Randall continued; "Pennery, are you quite sure that Kip told you everything that took place at Splash-Puddle that afternoon?"

"Absolutely certain. I can recall quite clearly... He told me in great detail."

"Yet he never mentioned he'd lost the knife?"

"No. he did not mention it. Because of course at that moment he thought it had just slipped out of its sheath, so in *his* mind it wasn't really lost because he knew where it would be and he'd recover it when it was light next day." Pennery paused: "On the other hand I'm now pretty sure he lost it when he says, because having given the matter thought, I've no recollection of seeing it after that day. I'd noticed it previously because he'd always worn it in the sheath on his belt." He hesitated, looking at Young Miss Parroty "I think it likely that he was anxious to find it before you asked him if it was... useful." They were all conscious of her habit of asking about the usefulness of her presents. She nodded, reluctant to admit any fact which threw doubt on Patterson's testimony.

"He told you about Pope Potter, but not that he'd lost his precious knife?" Patterson retorted sceptically. "That very first fire was at Splash-Puddle *and he was there the very day before!* Bathing?" He paused dramatically: "Or gathering holly and *building a fire to light the following evening!*"

"Well," Randall answered judicially, "if young Kip had been building a fire he would hardly have wanted to admit, let alone to draw attention to the fact that he'd ever been near Splash-Puddle." It was a telling point in the boy's favour.

"When I questioned the boys about the broken lace he said *nothing* about being *at* Splash-Puddle!" Patterson hurried on, once again glossing over the fact that he had never asked when any of them had last bathed there.

"And Kip *had* a *broken* lace?" Pennery waited. "Kip had *new* laces when you inspected the boys?" he persisted mildly.

Patterson hesitated: "No. Not exactly *new*, but they were both *unbroken* and most others had at least one broken, or joined."

"Was Kip the *only* boy with a pair of unbroken laces?"

"No, but..." The quiet way Pennery had made his point reduced Patterson to impotent fury. "I still..."

"Did you ask him if he *had* broken a lace and *had* replaced it?" Pennery persisted. Patterson remained mute. "So any boy having a pair of *unbroken* laces is a possible firebug?"

"The thing is, Leonard," Loxton put in somewhat ponderously, anxious to defuse the situation, "you were enquiring about the fire and trying to trace that broken lace...

what…two days was it after the fire? Now as far as I can remember *The Sentinel* had already gone on about the fire in a very big way. Even had they'd all been there at Splash-Puddle and even if you'd thought to ask them, would they have told you?" He turned to the others, "When we were kids, would any of us've owned-up to being at the very spot at the time the fire was being built?"

"I would have done," said Patterson loudly, then, sensing their frank disbelief, "I mean I *hope* I should have done."

"*I*, at that age," said Randall, "would probably have kept quiet," before pausing thoughtfully. "As kids often are when there's a row – too scared to say anything even if they're innocent."

"What about that evening you met him, Loxton?" The question from Patterson uncoiled across the room.

"That' does seem pretty damning at first in view of the fires later that night," Loxton admitted slowly, "at least in a way…" He screwed up his eyes in thought: "But is it really, I wonder? After all it tells us only that he was in the wood. And, y'know he'd've hardly had time to build *and then to light* four fires."

"Unless he'd prepared them *several days beforehand!*" Patterson interjected, eager to pounce on any weakness in Loxton's apparent extenuation of Kip's culpability.

"Wait a moment, Leonard," Randall interrupted sharply. "If you remember, the last of those fires had been lit only an hour before we got to it. The boy would have had to be out all night to set them all alight." He glanced across at Pennery.

"I can assure you he's always up and lively in the morning," Pennery responded.

"Still you must admit," Randall pointed out almost reluctantly, "if the boy *had* been out late that night, you might not have noticed that particular morning because you cancelled school for the day and slept in yourself."

"On the other hand…" Nodding slowly as he spoke, Loxton said, "Thinking back on that evening we met, Kip could easily have avoided me if he'd wanted to and I'd never have known he was anywhere in the area. But he came right up to me before I even knew he was there. Gave me quite a start! If he'd just been preparing fires, he'd surely have sneaked past without me being any the wiser."

"But what was he there for at all?" Young Miss Parroty interrupted shrilly, notebook poised.

"Looking for the knife you gave him," Pennery interpolated patiently. "That's what he told Patterson here when he was questioned about the knife."

"It looks as though you're trying to prove him to be innocent," Young Miss Parroty snapped icily.

"We're not here to *prove* anyone innocent or guilty, Miss Parroty," Loxton said in a fatherly way, "we just want to sort things out and discover who might have done what. If we can do that then we've done a good deal."

Miss Parroty drew in a loud breath.

"Then," Randall intervened hastily, seeing the light of battle in Miss Parrotys eye, "then of course there's the matter of the dog in the church."

They were all silent for a moment as they contemplated the horror of that situation.

"Was Kip at home that night?" Randall asked thoughtfully." After all, you were at Loxton's party."

"As far as I know he was," Pennery said, "I mean he was in for his supper before I went out and seemed to be his usual cheerful self. Of course I don't know what he was doing later when I wasn't there, but he was sound asleep when I returned and I'm sure he would have been noticeably disturbed if he'd just cut the throat of Pope Potter's dog. Anyhow and where had he got the beast from?" It was a question nobody had asked before.

Beginning to feel that his earlier theories had been too hastily propounded to convince them, Patterson broke in: "But now we know there were preparations behind the altar for a greenwood-smoke fire like the one at Splash-Puddle and we know he had been *there*. He was probably hiding behind the altar when you came in for organ practice, Eleanor?"

Randall intervened. "There's a point about the missing knife too. Miss Parroty, can you be sure when you last *saw* the knife with Kip, or when he last told you he still had it and was using it?"

"Well I...had that impression he was using it all the time so ..." Anxious as she was to support Patterson she had to admit that she could not recall the last time she had asked him. "Although I haven't actually *spoken* to him recently and..." her voice fading before adding speculatively, "I wonder whether he's been deliberately avoiding me?"

"Almost certainly," Patterson agreed, "because we now know that Mrs McKay was in his room the morning after we found the dog in the church and she discovered the empty sheath hidden in his sock drawer and," pausing significantly, "until now he's made no mention of losing it! Nor *where*," tapping first one finger on the table, "nor *when!*"

"It seems to me," Pennery said evenly, "that we must get hold of Pope Potter. It was his dog that was killed, the old fellow is probably distraught. Then, struck by a sudden thought, "Anybody seen him recently?" and very quietly, "Of course for all we know, somebody may have killed him too." After a moment's silence, "Furthermore Kip says he was at the pool... when he went to bathe and..." Patterson gave a disbelieving snort, which Pennery ignored, continuing, "and, if the boy really did leave his knife there, the old boy might well have picked it up." Finally, almost to himself, "Is the old boy mad enough to kill his own dog and...?"

"And is he still wandering around with the knife?" Randall voiced what they were all now thinking.

"Pennery's right," Loxton interrupted, anxious to quell any rumour of Pope Potter on a rampage, knife in hand. "After all, we're really blaming the kid, just because he's lost a knife. There's no other reason."

"Nonetheless," Randall reminded them, "it would appear that the killing of the dog and the fires may well be in some way connected. The kindling in the church is more than merely circumstantial evidence of some sort of connection with the other outbreaks."

"But it doesn't mean..." Loxton began heavily.

"That the person in question is Kip?" Randall finished for him. "No, I agree on that."

"Anyhow, where's the reason for it all? I mean there would have to have been a motive for a boy of eleven to behave in that way." Pennery offered the idea almost academically.

"He might not have been pleased that I wished to punish him for missing church," Patterson muttered. "I gather that you, Pennery, told him what I thought."

"He saw your letter if that's what you mean," Pennery answered, irritated by Patterson's pettiness, "but I had no wish to damn you in his eyes and I'm sure I didn't."

"How do we know he's telling the truth about Pope Potter being at the pool?" Elena Parroty sounded petulant. "I mean he could easily have invented the old man being there as a cover-up."

Loxton turned as a thought struck him. "Could it be that he was just putting the old man there in order to have a culprit for the fire he'd started?"

"I doubt any child could have made it up, it was so bizarre," Pennery replied."

"Something about the old loon splashing water at him?" Randall tried to recall what Patterson had told them.

"No, not exactly splashing, more like a christening. Apparently what happened was this." Pennery related everything Kip had told him in as much detail as he could remember.

There was an uncomfortable silence. Young Miss Parroty sat open-mouthed. "Do you mean to say that you *believe* that, Mr Pennery?"

"Why ever not?!" Pennery looked amused. "It's exactly what he told me."

"But Mr Pennery, why didn't you *do* something!"

"My dear Miss Parroty, what on earth should I have done? After all I wasn't there."

"Afterwards I mean. When he told you what had happened. You should have told Mr Randall! Of course you should. I mean if it's true then the man's…the man's…obviously the man's…"

"Deluded? Perhaps, but I'm sure he didn't do Kip any harm."

"Standing there in the water with a small boy who's… *in the nude*," Miss Parroty almost hissed the phrase. "He's obviously a S E X maniac." Her stage-whispered spelling of the word somehow exaggerated the obscenity of the scene she conjured up, which was not lost on the others who had done their best to dismiss the very same unwelcome suspicions. "I mean things like that *do* happen, don't they Mr Randall?"

"Things like that do indeed happen," Randall agreed reluctantly, "and I have to say I hadn't heard all this." Turning to the schoolmaster. "I must confess, Pennery, that I *am* a little surprised you didn't report it to me officially."

"I thought the less fuss the better. It was only something of a joke to the boy. I thought it best left like that. I am quite certain from Kip's attitude that there was no attempt to molest him in the way Miss Parroty is suggesting." Pennery sighed, "Why confuse an eleven-year-old by suggesting sinister interpretations when clearly he saw none? Guilt, like beauty you know, lies in the eye of the beholder."

"*I* would certainly have taken action, had *I* been appointed the boy's *official* guardian and he'd told me what he told you," Patterson said smugly. "*Vice, 'We first endure'* as the poet Dryden put it, '*then pity, then embrace'.*"

"Alexander Pope, *not* Dryden." Pennery retorted, stung by Patterson's complacency. "Anyhow for what it's worth I, as Kip's *appointed* guardian am quite certain that the boy hadn't been 'indecently assaulted' in any way. If there had been anything like that I am sure he would have told me. As far as I can see the old madman was practising at being some sort of latter-day John the Baptist."

Loxton, satisfied by Pennery's certainty that the incident, although definitely odd, was not criminal, said breezily, "What matters is that it seems the old boy really was there and it doesn't look as though Kip came to any harm. I mean it's not as if the boy said the old coot tickled his ba...or anything," he ended lamely, blushing to the tips of his ears.

In the astonished hush, Miss Parroty squeaked and relapsed into silence. Patterson decided to look disapproving. Randall gave Loxton a half-amused old-fashioned look, as much as to say *that's another gaffe you'll not live down, Henry!*

Pennery laughed, which eased the tension. "That about it, then? Can we go?" Then with a light touch of irony, "I take it, Dill, that you don't yet feel it necessary to lock up young Kip?"

"No, just keep an eye on him. However, it occurs to me, as it must do to all of you, that *if* Pope Potter had molested him, then the boy might have killed the dog in retaliation. And if he also bitterly resented Patterson's letter why not do it in the church? Two birds with one stone so to speak, but why on earth would he want to set fires all over the forest? However, I have to say he just doesn't seem to me to be that sort of youngster. I've seen nothing at all in Kip Harrison's behaviour to suggest him being responsible for anything like that."

Patterson, intractably unconvinced of Kip's innocence as he was, snorted his dismissal of Randall's reservations, but Loxton having recovered his composure, sought to defuse the situation: "Furthermore, Dill I'm quite certain that Pennery here would have noticed some change in the boy's demeanour if he'd been involved in anything as brutal as the death of the dog, or as dangerous as setting off fires in the forest."

With the exception of Patterson and his acolyte Young Miss Parroty who, profoundly shocked by Loxton's vulgarity, had remained mute (mischievously Pennery wondered if she would ever speak again) none of them could genuinely believe the polite, biddable boy they had come to know and like over the three years he had been with them was capable of threatening their lives by lighting fires, let alone slitting the throat of a dog.

Loxton decided to end the meeting. "I suggest we adjourn the discussion for the time being. Above all we need to find Pope Potter and question him…(*if he is still alive* hung unspoken in the air) but that may have to wait until The Great Blaze is finally extinguished."

That evening Pennery, thinking to reassure Kip, gave him a careful *résumé*.

"But Mr Pennery, do they all *really* believe I didn't do it? Any of it?"

"I think so."

"Even Mr Patterson? And Miss Parroty?" Sensing Pennery's indecision, the boy persisted, "They would *all* believe me if they knew I really *had* lost my knife and Pope Potter had it all the time, wouldn't they?"

"I wouldn't worry, but yes, you know I think even Miss Parroty would believe you if they realised he'd found your knife that time at Splash-Puddle. But don't go looking for him."

"*You* believe me anyhow, don't you?"

"Yes," hesitating fractionally, "yes, Kip, I think I do."

Even as he heard himself, Pennery knew he needed to sound less judicial and turned to place a comforting hand on Kip's shoulder but the boy had already slipped away and with him went the opportunity to assure his ward that he was always on his side.

16

i

The last phase began about ten in the morning. Wind returned, gentle at first but becoming increasingly stronger, thrusting The Great Blaze forward again at a smart pace; the unfinished firebreak was overwhelmed in a few hours. A large area with particularly thick, parched undergrowth allowed it to advance far more quickly than hitherto; vanguard of an invading army, tongues of flame sneaked ahead firing individual trees as if inviting in the main conflagration and welcoming its arrival.

The military units began to retreat once more. One contingent stopped off to supplement the remaining Salter's Creek firefighters, but the rest withdrew fifty miles to the east, where a massive final operation was underway, clearing vast areas in an attempt finally to halt The Great Blaze before it encroached on suburban outskirts of Cranston. Already wide expanses had been reduced to blackened stumps where nothing stirred. Unknown to the fleeing men and women of the farmsteads, black and white cine-film of The Great Blaze had become world news. Grainy sequences of trucks packed with refugees clutching the pathetic remnants of their possessions featured in every cinema. Newspapers headlined dire predictions, their front pages featuring dramatic photographs of animals fleeing before the flames. It was by far the biggest forest fire anyone could recall: the Prime Minister declared a National Emergency.

Despite the fact that Salter's Creek on its treeless rocky knoll had, in the past, been unaffected by forest fires other than suffering a cindery smoke-laden atmosphere, Loxton and Randall wondered again about encouraging, even ordering most of the remaining families to move out even though the road was already overcrowded with vehicles of all descriptions. Kennethina Biggelow already departed, now it was reported that Mr Soong had vanished. Outside the laundry, well protected from falling smuts, the washing he had completed was parcelled up, neatly labelled ready for collection beside the door on which the notice, **CLOSED**, gave no indication of where he had gone or when, if ever, he might return.

Then, miraculously, the brisk wind subsided into a steady but gentle breeze. Furthermore a new weather forecast predicting heavy rain gave hope that the ordeal was at an end. On these two counts they decided they could give themselves until Saturday before ordering evacuation if that still seemed necessary.

About five o'clock in the evening there came an alarm call from the duty observer in the tower at Three Pine Rough. Puffs of smoke had been spotted, once again from a fire to the east of Salter's Creek. The on-call team raced to the location and managed to put it out before it took hold, but smouldering rags and careful arrangement of dry undergrowth told their own tale. At seven in the evening there came another call, then another, until all three squads as well as the remaining military personnel were out. Whilst they were away two other blazes began and a little later two more, all to the east, confirming Randall's earlier suspicion: the firebug intended to prevent any escape to the east. Before midnight the new blaze was out of control and just before dawn the road east was finally cut: evacuating Salter's Creek was now an impossibility.

As daylight strengthened the firefighters, including the remaining soldiers, gave up attempting to do more, trooping back dirty, dog-tired, demoralised. Despite their awareness of the historic invulnerability of Salter's Creek, for the first time ever the inhabitants became fearful of imminent immolation. Even at that early hour there were women and children dowsing sparks and glowing cinders.

Like puppies chasing each other's tails, the flames to the west of them were driven much closer by the very same breeze which was pushing fires to the east further away, no longer could there be any doubt that these too had been deliberately started. There was still no sign of the forecast rain.

At breakfast time the breeze mercifully lessened further. However even though The Great Blaze chewed its way more slowly from the west, it allowed the eastern blaze to begin to eat its way inexorably back towards them. By midday the two advancing fires had joined together to the south. It was only a matter of hours before the same happened in the rough thick undergrowth to the north; Salter's Creek was encircled. Although islanded by its comparative barrenness the centre would be safe from the advancing flames, increasing quantities of still-glowing airborne embers threatened to ignite decades-dry never-completed dwellings on the embryonic streets flanking McCutcheon Square; buckets filled with water lining the sidewalks as precaution against this very contingency seemed pathetically inadequate.

To all intents and purposes the sun remained an angry red moon, dimly visible through thick smoke. Coughing and wheezing, the last women and children from outlying settlements thronged the square and embryonic streets, unpredictable up-current of hot air lifting hats and skirts.

Pennery had abandoned any pretence of schooling, offering instead temporary accommodation on the floor of Big Schoolroom to pupils and their families fleeing from outlying farmsteads, who were now trapped in Salter's Creek. The choking, throat tearing atmosphere seemed to be sucking all life-giving oxygen from the very air he breathed. Gas?... *Back in the trenches again?... "GAS!...GAS!...GAAAAAS..."*

As daylight faded, the surrounding glow lit up the darkness like gigantic blood-red floodlights. Rogerson had stubbornly insisted on going back to rescue what he could before flames finally engulfed their home; he did not re-appear. First Randall, then Loxton and finally his despairing family were forced to realise that he had choked and scorched to death somewhere in the inferno. It was the first fatality.

Flames were now licking at the last trees hardly three miles from the town's outer boundary: the air already hotter and heavier, smuts and cinders falling like black hail, a dull roar as of a distant ocean pummelling the ear. Although the wind remained down, the slow advance of The Great Blaze seemed ever more relentless, even more menacing, than its previous, gale-driven, helter-skelter, almost skittish rush forward. It played with their fears as a cat might play with a mortally wounded mouse, apparently dying down before springing back brighter, hotter, fiercer from not quite the same place.

Further precautions were taken. From the few remaining cars, wheels were removed, air let from the tyres which were stored where they could not be fire-damaged. Petrol tanks were drained into cans and, together with a number of large drums of fuel, stored deep underground; at least the emergency vehicles might be able to move as soon as the road was passable. Cars were jacked up and corralled under constant watch in McCutcheon Square – the point furthest from the flames. Abandoned houses and verandas had been regularly hosed until, unused to so much water, wood swelled and sidewalk boards became soggy. Water was stored in every available domestic container including baths in order to be able dowse sparks immediately wherever they fell. Two old, very dry little-used wooden barns behind Parrotys Store were demolished. Salter's Creek put itself into a state of siege and settled down to wait. The flames, in no hurry, were prepared to take their time, prowling like lurking predators here and there, wherever they chose, as if seeking weaknesses in the perimeter.

Randall climbed the watchtower tower in Three Pine Rough. They no longer felt the need to have it constantly manned by watchers as there was no point in their exhausted emergency squads setting out to remedy what far larger military resources failed to achieve.

It was a fine viewpoint. Like incoming tide surrounding a sandcastle, the flames crept ineluctably on. Dribbles of fire reached surreptitiously out into the decreasing perimeter until the last few remaining trees exploded into flame. More distantly the angry red louring sky had dulled into orange while, even further away, below dense black clouds from which hung udders of dirty white smoke, the orange had sullenly subsided into a pale resentful pink. Although he knew that the township itself could never be overwhelmed, it was nonetheless a terrifying spectacle. He watched for what seemed only minutes but when he returned to the ground he found he had been up there for hours.

At the bottom of the wooden laddering he met the Minister. In the stress of the impending disaster, Patterson's usual animosity was absent. "We'll just have to sit it out. We shall pray for rain."

Won't make much difference anyhow, Randall thought to himself but said, "It might mean we can get most of the women and children out if your prayers are successful tomorrow."

"Today," Patterson said, oblivious of Randall's ironic tone. "It's Sunday now."

Looking at his watch, Randall saw that it was not only Sunday, but almost five o'clock in the morning, hanging smoke making it virtually impossible any longer to tell night from day. "Even so, it'll be days before the ground has cooled sufficiently for anyone to get away."

"That's what I meant," Patterson went on. "That's what I mean, we must pray for rain to quench the fire *and* cool the ground. I've just heard on the radio that they were having very heavy thunderstorms all night on the east coast. We must pray the storms move west."

ii

Pennery returned to the school, eventually dozing off into a restless slumber, the smut-laden air making breathing painful. Even Kip, who had slept through with windows shut, woke with rasping throat on the day of Joyce Patterson's address. Because everyone had been up so much of the night before, it was fortunate Patterson had decreed church services should be held in the evening rather than the morning.

"I expect *everyone* will be in church today."

Kip breathing softly to ease aching tonsils, understood Pennery meant that they should go too, *both* of them. Even Pope Potter was amongst the crowd outside, an object of passing curiosity to people far too tired and anxious at the way Fate had treated them to do anything more than stare. Randall decided to catch him at the end of the service. Kip glimpsed him as they entered and he too determined to tackle him afterwards. However, in the confusion which terminated the occasion Pope Potter disappeared before either Randall or Kip could confront him.

Throughout the day tension had heightened as the smouldering fire had crept closer. Inside the church, even though curiously muted, the distant roar of The Great Blaze jarred the ear, as if the organ had stuck on one low, growling, menacing note. Patterson had not forgotten about his wife's 'sermon' but, because of the crisis, had assumed she would want him to speak instead of her, particularly in view of Rogerson's presumed death. Did his family still hope? None of them had even been seen to cry, though it was impossible that he could ever have survived that inferno. Rogerson had always organised older children to gather greenery to decorate the church for Christmas carols, to bring fruit and flowers for harvest festivals. However, much to Patterson's surprise, Joyce was steely, adamant, almost aggressively so and this, together with his own rasping-throated weariness, decided him to let her have her way. He would take the opportunity to say something to comfort the Rogerson family immediately after her brief tribute to Margaret Clitherow, just before the closing hymn. Had he been less exhausted he might have wondered why, in the stifling heat and smoke-filled air, she chose to wear her all-enveloping winter fur coat.

An exceptionally over-long hymn was sung while Loxton took the Collection. Pennery was not alone in feeling it was a in some way a memorial service for a Salter's Creek that had gone for ever: the last vestiges of a frontier way of life were vanishing with the trees, which had for so long held at bay an increasingly inquisitive, intrusive, outside world. Everyone supposed they would live through the present crisis but there was a despairing communal weariness of soul: what had they done to deserve this? Would the struggle to rebuild cindered homesteads and re-cultivate incinerated fields be worth the effort when this holocaust could all happen again?

The organ stopped, the Collection was received at the altar by Patterson. The church grew silent except for people coughing and the distant roar of the fire (Was it fainter? Had the wind dropped altogether?) Clutching her fur coat about her, Joyce Patterson, revealing that she was wearing startlingly bright red high-heeled shoes, ascended the rickety steps to the pulpit slowly, as if painfully aware of their hazardous state. Loxton crossed his fingers: *We really ought to have done something about them, Patterson's been on about it for ages.* She pushed through the waist-high 'stable-door' into the pulpit and, as if in retaliation for its neglect, the one remaining dry-rotted peg that secured them resigned all responsibility and the steps clattered to the floor.

"Later," she commanded a boy in the front pew who darted forward to try to replace them.

On previous occasions, she had never taken a text, but spoken briefly, simply and fluently of the Elizabethan martyr so dear to her heart and the reason for seeking her canonisation. A listless congregation, minds on the menace of the surrounding fires, shifted themselves into a polite semblance of interest as she opened the great Bible which somehow dominated the pulpit.

"The cry of Sodom and Gomorrah is multiplied, their sin become exceeding grievous. And the Lord rained upon Sodom and Gomorrah brimstone *AND FIRE* from out of Heaven."

Quite apart from the astonishing text she had chosen her whole manner, hands tight on the edge of the pulpit, riveted Pennery's attention. *She's on the verge of a break-down.* The congregation, hypnotized by her intensity, sat as if turned to stone.

"Of course," Joyce Patterson declaimed, "you know IT'S *NOT*

TRUE. What *they* are saying IS. NOT. TRUE." Pennery was not alone in wondering who *they* were and what it was *they* were saying. "Don't believe what *they* say. Oh, I know all about the meetings behind locked doors and *What They Say* but it's not true. Not about Leonard. He's not like that. No! Oh no, not like that at all. *He*. Likes. *Women*." She leaned further forward, hair falling about her face, laughing triumphantly. "Do you know what he's like in bed? With women? I do. He's *splendid* in bed."

Silence unnervingly profound. Already diminished, the roar of the fire seemed to have faded altogether as if it too was astonished into silence. "Leonard knows what to do." She nodded confidentially, "I can't give him all he wants," knowingly, grotesquely. "He has to have other women too. I don't mind at all." She looked round the congregation pointedly; "Miss Parroty doesn't mind either." There came strangled yelp followed by a loud squawk as Young Miss Parroty jammed her hands on the organ keys in her agitation. Patterson stupefied, unable to believe what he was hearing, sat as stunned as the rest of the congregation.

"Of course it was different with the boy. *He* wanted Leonard to do it, but then Leonard wouldn't." She leaned over the pulpit, "You know it was the boy who killed the dog in the church here? Oh yes! Yes! Yes! Yes it was. I *know*. He threw the knife away afterwards. Do you know how I know?" She looked meaningfully back at the altar. "God Told Me, He sent His Angel at ten-fifteen this morning." Confidentially, "I was in the bath, but I didn't mind an Angel." She leaned over the pulpit: "Do you know why the boy killed the dog?" Patterson had begun to move, struggling to erect the fallen steps. Pennery, realising what she was about to imply, had already hurried Kip from the church telling him to find the doctor and he now ran back down the aisle to help.

"Because—" she leaned over, leering horribly, confidentially "—listen, I'll tell you." She beckoned. "Because of course in

the woods…At Splash-Puddle…the old man…*buggered him…*"
There came a long gasp from the congregation. Almost as one it
unfroze; young and old, jamming each other in the pews choking
the aisle behind Pennery, they stumbled for the doors which,
mercifully, had been left wide open on account of the heat.

"The Angel told me." She nodded confidentially. "Said it came
from God Himself…Leonard's not like that…Leonard's not like
that…*GOD. Says. Leonard. Didn't. Do. It*" raising her gaze to the
roof as if confident the Angel, even God himself would manifest
his presence there and then in wholehearted agreement.

Pennery and Patterson were having difficulty with the steps
which had broken apart in their collapse. Finally registering the
implication of the words she was using to defend him, Patterson
shouted, "Why doesn't that damned Parroty drown her out
with the organ?!" It was the first time he had ever sworn, let
alone in church so intent was he on stopping his wife as, to his
utter disbelief she produced a bottle of what he recognised as
Communion wine and took three long swigs.

"Oh and another thing," Joyce Patterson continued but now
in a chatty, social voice, "There was That Sign From God. Much
earlier. Before the dog. Those ants at the boy's party. They
were the same as the Plagues in Egypt you know, a warning
to us all." She dropped her voice theatrically, like a music-hall
comedian about to tell a blue joke. "The boy caused the ants."
Taking another swig, "Ants in our pants… All together now…"
She began to sing and conduct as if leading a nursery rhyme
for a class of small children. "Ant-ses in our pant-ses! An'ses' in-
our-*pan*-ses!" Then, draining the bottle with another couple of
swigs, giggling helplessly, deposited it with bizarre carefulness
over the side of the pulpit where it smashed on the floor beside
her mortified husband, and began to chant, "An-tics in our pan-
tics… *I've* got an-tics in my pan-tics. They tickle and make me
fran-tics. Look!"

As if a striptease *artiste*, very slowly, button by button, she began to shed the fur coat. Finally with a flourish she cast it down into the now-empty front pew. She wore nothing beneath it. Patterson stood speechless, appalled. The last few stalwarts who had delayed wondering whether they could be of help turned and fled.

At long last, the organ sounded, handfuls of wrong notes perhaps, but loud and discordant enough to drown her out. Unable to placate her, Loxton and Randall, having fought their way through the last of the dumbstruck outgoing congregation together with Pennery hauled her from the pulpit still mouthing obscenities, stark-naked except for silk stockings, black suspenders and very high-heeled bright red shoes.

Kip had located Doctor Svenssen who, having hastened to Salter's Creek to tend burns and minor injuries of refugees from the outlying farmsteads shortly before the road back east became impassable, was fortunately still on hand. It took all four of them to restrain her whilst he gave her an injection.

17

It became a night of rumour. Who had killed the dog and why? Why had The Great Blaze burned so fiercely and for so long? What reason was there for the march of the ants? Who had set the fires alight? There was no rational explanation for the disaster which had overtaken the community, none whatever. These and other half-formulated, even totally imaginary, fears had been touched off afresh by Joyce Patterson. Insane though Patterson's wife might be, she had somehow allowed credibility to hitherto nagging but indefinable uncertainties which nourished anxiety. Misinformation was rife: Young Miss Parroty, frightened by the ravings which had connected her name with Patterson, doing what she believed was right, sorting, as she thought, the husk from the grain of Joyce Patterson's mad sermon, hinting that evidence suggested Kip Harrison might be both *and* dog-killer. Fraught minds remembering old gossip, rumour evolved into half-truth, half-fiction. A few, long-tutored by superstitious religiosity, selecting the phrases they wanted to hear and which supported their prejudices from the wife of the Minister, convinced themselves that the fires, like plague of ants, were signs of Divine Displeasure brought down on them by Pennery's refusal to punish the Smokers because, had he excluded Kip Harrison, it would have revealed the unnatural partiality of a pæderastic schoolmaster for his young catamite.

Randall did his best to dispel these whispers and quash the gossip that gave them currency, increasingly convinced that the one person who might throw some light on the matter was Pope Potter who was not dead as many had supposed. He had spotted him in the vicinity of the church the previous day, although whether he had been inside and had heard Joyce Patterson's diatribe nobody could be certain. In the morning he would no doubt locate the old man somewhere amongst those who had fled from the surrounding settlements to the safety of Salter's Creek which was now completely islanded within the encirclement of still-scorching ground and smouldering tree trunks.

Questioning the preacher was certainly a matter of importance, however, in their immediate besieged circumstances, not prime importance. Although events had moved too swiftly for people to reflect on what they said in the stress of the moment most, but by no means all of them, had subsequently qualified their earlier utterances; in their heart of hearts they did not believe the tragically bereaved youngster they had come to know and cherish could be responsible for the fires, nor the slaughter of the dog – especially that. Randall regarded the suspicions stirred by the garrulous Miss Parroty, neither strong enough nor yet organised enough to warrant him detaining Kip for his own safety. *On the other hand if, as Joyce Paterson had implied, the old man had molested the boy who had retaliated by... .* He must certainly, question Kip far more closely at the first opportunity.

Every so often the fitful wind showered a house or outbuilding with sparks and embers which needed to be dowsed immediately by ever-vigilant men and women. United in the common cause, Kip, who with other children, carried food and flasks of tea, was becoming aware of what was being whispered. Although understanding little of what Mrs Patterson had implied before Pennery had hustled him out of church to fetch Dr Svenssen, it seemed that he was being held responsible not only for the fires but, because he had lost his knife, for the death of the dog too. It was well after midnight when, utterly exhausted, he staggered home, fell into bed in smoke-reeking clothes and was instantly asleep.

Grimy figures still hurried through drifts of smoke, scarves across their mouths replenishing buckets. Now, in the murky Monday dawn light, it seemed suddenly to be large soft black cinders, rather than sparks pattering down like black snow onto tin roof and car top; at first bystanders seemed unable to comprehend the significance of the spreading patches in the dust.

"RAIN?"

A single hoarse voice.

"The rain's come to put out The Great Blaze."

News spread as rapidly as had the flames themselves: doors banged, windows rattled, hooters were hooted. Pennery had never made it back to the school, he Randall and Loxton had stayed with Patterson who, dazed with shock, had hardly spoken since they had sedated his wife and tied her to the bed. The racket first aroused the schoolmaster who had dozed off in a chair "Henry! Henry!" He shook Loxton who lay on the sofa deep asleep. "Henry, I think it's begun to rain!"

They hastened to the door where they were joined by Randall. Miraculous black drops, individual and occasional they may have been, but they continued to fall with increasing frequency, spreading and joining in the dust.

"Thank God!" Loxton stood in his doorway. "Thank God the summer's over."

Speechlessly, Patterson appeared, ashen face sunk and lined, shoes unlaced, dressing gown over hastily donned shirt and trousers, suddenly a very old man.

Pennery held up his hand! "Isn't that an *organ* playing somewhere?"

It was. Very loud. *Amplified?*

"Pope Potter!" muttered Randall, who had woken to find himself convinced of the old preacher's involvement. "I believe that old bastard has had *everything* to do with those fires," hurrying out purposefully.

"Does he indeed?" Patterson growled savagely, glaring round at Pennery with smouldering eyes, spitting out, "Now even *he's* making excuses for that boy. *Just like you!*"

Pennery opened his mouth then, thinking better of his intended retort, said mildly, "Let's find out, shall we? Let's at least give Kip the benefit of the doubt until we've had time to question that mad old coot."

Patterson's eyes, already losing their anger, became dull, listless. Randall ran back shouting to Loxton and Pennery, "Pope Potter has…"

"What has he said about Kip and the knife?"

"I don't know."

"Didn't you…?"

"You'll see… . Come on, Three Pines Rough…" Randall panted, and dashed out again.

"Three Pines…?" Pennery and Loxton looked at each other and set off after him. Patterson followed, dressing gown flapping cassock-like round him.

Kip too was woken by the hooting and shouting. Having fallen asleep without having even taken off his shoes he was outside in seconds. Pennery he supposed was still fire-fighting with other adults. Suddenly, loudspeakers from Three Pine Rough started to boom. *But there was no longer any need to have watchers up there?* Something familiar made him stop, listen and then run in that direction.

"Sorry. the rain's come, firebug?" an adult voice laughed.

Although last night such teasing by his contemporaries might have been meant in fun, he was aware that adults were now joining in. Unaccustomed as he was to analysing intonations, he nevertheless sensed that, in their relief that the rain had come at last and, in the growing daylight increasingly aware of the devastating legacy of The Great Blaze, they really had started blaming him for the catastrophe.

Certain that Pope Potter must have found his knife, Kip ran faster. Surely the preacher would tell everyone that he, Kip, had never built the fire at Splash Puddle? After summoning Dr Svenssen, he had hoped to have a chance to speak to the old man and, in view of Pennery's warning, with plenty of people about, but he never even glimpsed him in the confusion of the mass 'evacuation' triggered by Mrs Patterson's rant. Now he knew where to find Pope Potter.

"Goin' ter kill another dog?" a voice yelled out.

Spurred by the taunts, he determined to tackle the preacher face to face – *Above all, mus' convince Mister Pennery I'd nothing to do with the fires or killing the dog.*

At Three Pine Rough a fast-growing crowd stared-up at Pope Potter on the platform. He had used the pulley system to haul up the harmonium-altar. Bereft of its load, the abandoned tricycle waited patiently below.

The music suddenly stopped. "Sin Is…" boomed the voice. Electric leads loosened by the wind, the loudspeakers hummed and crackled, words kept disappearing, "Sin …Died…New Life Is Come." A crackling hiss, the voice faded. It began to rain much harder. Already drifts of acid-smelling white steam were beginning to mix with the smoke.

"It's like the last acts of a black comedy," Pennery said more to himself than anyone else. "We'll have to wait till he comes down to question him."

A small figure moved out of the crowd and towards the tree.

"Good God!" There was alarm in Loxton's voice. "That's the boy. He's going to climb up there to talk to the old fool!" He and Randall began to run towards Kip but they were far too late. Already Kip was twenty feet away and climbing quickly. Panting they stood at the foot of the tree looking up.

"Come down, Kip! Leave it till he comes down!"

"I really did *lose* my knife." He climbed another step, stopped. "I mus' get him to tell *them*," nodding at the crowd, before looking down directly at Pennery and adding quietly, 'An' to tell *you*, 'cos you mus' believe me, Mister Pennery, I di'n't do the fires or..or.. *anythin'* to his dog."

"I do believe you Kip. *Of course* you didn't!"

"I also am quite sure you didn't," Randall bellowed, "so come down, please Kip, come down."

"I want *him* to tell *everyone* that it wasn't *me*." He looked up at the platform, then nodding down once again at the now-silenced crowd of onlookers, 'An' *they*, won't really believe me till they hear him tell them I *never* built a fire that night at Splash-Puddle," Then, hesitating before moving on up, 'An' I'm sure it must be him who found my knife."

"Get him down, Pennery!" Patterson called. "*You* are *supposed* to be the boy's guardian."

Stung by reference to the responsibility of his guardianship, Pennery said with as much self-restraint as he could muster, "Can't you see he won't come down?"

"Then *I'll* get him." Randall moved forward.

"No!" Loxton stopped the policeman. "There's only danger if the old man gets violent. He won't if it's just the boy up there."

At a slower pace, Kip reached the top. It was higher than he had thought. Then, with a heave he was on the platform. Below, they all stood back to see what happened.

"They'll be all right as long as they keep still," Pennery said as if to echo Loxton.

The old man, hair lifted by the wind into a monstrous grey halo, turned and saw the boy. The loudspeakers burst into life, now without crackling interruptions. "Ahhhhhhh! *He* Comes! The Prince of Light. Fire Shall Consume The World at The End and The Lion And The Ox Shall Bend The Knee At The Coming of The Prince of Light. See! See!" The old man, in billowing robes which appeared to have been washed by the now drenching rain, stretched out an arm: "See how God has Eaten up the Sinful World in Righteous Flame as the Prince of Light Comes Into His Kingdom." The harsh voice boomed out, eerily amplified in the damp smoke-filled air.

He moved towards the boy. The crowd held its breath. Reverently from his harmonium-altar he lifted something... *Holly?* A wreath? Taking up his bean-tin chalice with his other hand he poured something over the boy's already damp hair. Kip stood transfixed as the old man placed the crown on his head, red berries bright as blood against the thorny dark green leaves.

"*THIS ABOMINATION MUST STOP!*" Patterson, features convulsed as they had been the evening they had discovered the murdered dog, pushed himself forward.

Pennery tried to catch his arm, calling urgently, "It'll stop when he's said what he has to say."

"It must stop *now*. It is *BLASPHEMY*. I shall stop it!"

"You saw me that time at Splash-Puddle, di'n't you Mr Potter?" Kip's high voice tense and frightened sounded over the speakers. "You saw me, didn't you? You saw that I never built any fire?" The patent sincerity in his voice convinced those below more effectively than any answer of Pope Potter's.

"I Christened You on Jordan's Bank. Now the Waters which

Anointed you flow back to Cleanse the Sin-filled Earth," pointing up into the teeming rain. "And the Hour is at Hand of the Coming of God *Your* Father." The voice pitched even higher than Kip's into a chant. "The Hour had Come and *Your* Servant has sent *Your* Sign to the Four Corners of the Sinful Earth and Summon the Horsemen on their Fiery steeds. *I Rode with Them in Your Chariot of Fire. SATAN. IS. SLAIN!"*

Patterson seemed rooted to the ground... *SATAN IS SLAIN...?* Had he not once rebuked the old man..."*Not even a dumb animal deserved such a reviled name...*" his own condemnatory words whirling in his head.

At that moment, a crack of thunder, a shaft of lightening illuminated the whole sky and, in that instant, as if it had enlightened him too, he understood: the boy was entirely innocent, had nothing to do with the fires, or with the desecration of his church. He, Leonard Patterson, had allowed his feud with Pennery to blind him to his Christian duty. But now! Now the Good Lord in His infinite mercy had presented him with the opportunity to redeem himself! He would climb up there, confront the old man, reassure the boy, use the loudspeakers to confirm the boy's innocence, confess to them all that allegations he himself had made were totally without foundation. He would acknowledge publically his failure as their Minister, beg them to absolve him for his lack of compassion. Although they would surely realise an error was understandable in the circumstances? As if God himself was condemning his moral self-deception there came a second reverberating crack of thunder... *NO...not an understandable error...* followed by a third *...NO-O-O...your unforgivable sin.*

Patterson wrenched himself free, throwing off both Loxton and Pennery and ran towards the ladder. They recovered and sought to climb after him but he turned and stamped his heels on their fingers. "This is a great blasphemy," he shouted and, now on the second ladder, Patterson kicked the lower one free of its hooks. Those immediately below jumped hastily back and watched him climb on. He went slowly for the rain still fell and the worn wooden rungs were slippery.

Randall stood with his back to the tree, a foot on the fallen ladder. "Nobody else" he said quietly, "the platform is intended only for two."

Kip and Pope Potter appeared not to have moved as Patterson heaved himself onto the platform. Pope Potter continued chanting.

"*Stop that...OBSCENITY!*"

Pope Potter took no notice. Kip clutched Patterson, frightened, not of the height but of the hostility of people who believed he had killed the dog, had started the fires and above all, by a sense of utter desolation: *even Mr Pennery doubted him.* Patterson put a reassuring hand on the boy's shoulder. He looked around him. The white-draped top of the Old Man's harmonium-altar was complete with its clock; beside it a horn-handled knife, blade black with dried blood.

"Let us Worship the Prince of Light!" Taking up the knife and holding it aloft, the old man eyed Kip: "Thus with the Instrument *Thou* Gavest Me was The Prince of Darkness slain."

"I didn't *give* you my knife. You *took* it." High pitched with indignation, his voice rang out from the speakers.

"I your Servant am About Your Father's Business!"

Arm still round Kip, overcome by blind hatred for the blaspheming old man, Patterson tried to seize the knife but, thwarted by Pope Potter, shouted, "This...*abomination*..." and swept the cloth from the harmonium. In a sudden silence from the amplifiers, the displaced clock exploded like a bomb on the rocky ground beneath.

"Let's go down, Kip." The loudspeakers live once more conveyed uncharacteristic gentleness in Patterson's tone.

"Who Dares Desecrate His Altar? Who would take The Prince of Light from this His Realm of Air?" The old man's amplified words bellowed out as he lurched forward, his other hand clutching for the boy.

Kip, now genuinely terrified, pulled himself closer against Patterson, who shoved the old man off. Pope Potter staggered back against the harmonium which slowly slithered across the soaking platform. Petrified, all three of them watched the flimsy guard-rail give way. The harmonium vanished with a chilling shriek as the chain to which it was still attached flailed through ungreased pulley-wheels faster than ever intended. It was almost at the bottom, when the chain jammed fast. There came a shuddering jolt. One of its securing pegs dislodged by the sudden weight of the harmonium, the platform tilted. A second peg popped out like a champagne cork, then a third, the platform tilting further each time as the harmonium bounced bizarrely at the end of the chain.

"Watch out! Watch out, it's tipping right over!" Patterson heard himself shout; the microphone catching his words, amplified them into a despairing scream.

Another jolt, another peg free and the chain finally snapping, the harmonium shattered on the waiting rocks as the platform lurched violently to an even more impossible angle.

White-robed, hands raised, still holding the knife, Pope Potter slithered past them, stopped only momentarily by the jagged remains of the guardrail. Patterson felt himself sliding on a floor which seemed to be disappearing from beneath his feet. In an instinctive attempt at self-preservation, entirely forgetting the boy he had been holding, he flung out both arms wrapping them around one of the three supporting trees. Kip in his flimsy rubber-soled sneakers stood no chance on the steep rain-slicked surface. In a vain attempt to save himself by grasping another of the supporting trees he too flung his arms wide.

Those below stood transfixed.

Except for Pennery.

In that moment, recognising at last how casually he had accepted his responsibilities, he acknowledged for the first time the duties, the obligations of the guardianship so haphazardly thrust upon him. He sprang forward, arms extended, hoping against hope that, even if not in time to catch Kip completely, he might at least lessen his impact on the unforgiving ground. Stumbling over the broken body of Pope Potter, Pennery looked up into the eyes of a boy crowned with thorns floating towards him, arms outspread as if attempting to fly…yearning for his guardian's embrace? Or preparing for crucifixion.

Lightning Source UK Ltd.
Milton Keynes UK
UKHW022327131118
332305UK00005B/239/P